DOCTOR WHO
AND THE
GENESIS OF THE DALEKS

THE CHANGING FACE OF DOCTOR WHO
The cover illustration portrays the Fourth Doctor whose
physical appearance later changed after he fell from a radio
telescope saving the universe.

DOCTOR WHO
AND THE
GENESIS OF THE DALEKS

Based on the BBC Television serial *Genesis of the Daleks* by Terry Nation by arrangement with the BBC

TERRANCE DICKS

BOOKS

9 10 8

BBC Books, an imprint of Ebury Publishing
20 Vauxhall Bridge Road,
London SW1V 2SA

BBC Books is part of the Penguin Random House group of companies
whose addresses can be found at global.penguinrandomhouse.com

Novelisation copyright © Terrance Dicks 1976
Original script © Terry Nation 1975
The Changing Face of Doctor Who and About the
Author © Justin Richards 2015
Daleks created by Terry Nation

Published by BBC Books in 2016
First published in 1976 by Universal-Tandem Publishing Co. Ltd.

www.eburypublishing.co.uk

A CIP catalogue record for this book is available from the British Library

ISBN 978 1 785 94038 5

Editorial Director: Albert DePetrillo
Editorial Manager: Grace Paul
Series Consultant: Justin Richards
Cover design: Lee Binding © Woodlands Books Ltd, 2016
Cover illustration: Chris Achilleos
Production: Alex Goddard

Printed and bound in Great Britain by Clays Ltd, Elcograf S.p.A.

Typeset in India by Thomson Digital Pvt Ltd, Noida, Delhi

Penguin Random House is committed to a sustainable future for
our business, our readers and our planet. This book is made from
Forest Stewardship Council® certified paper.

Contents

Contents

The Changing Face of Doctor Who

The Fourth Doctor

This *Doctor Who* novel features the fourth incarnation of the Doctor. In this incarnation, the Doctor seemed more alien than ever. He was a constant surprise to his enemies and to his companions.

Instantly recognisable in his floppy hat and long scarf, the Doctor became less authoritarian and aristocratic than his predecessor. This Doctor was a rebel as well as a hero. He was Renaissance Man made real – a Jack of all trades and master of all of them. And, for all his alien mutability and Olympian detachment, the Fourth Doctor could be the most 'human' of Doctors.

But, as with the Second Doctor, there was an air of superficiality to much of his banter and play-acting. It is in the quieter moments, the deeper moments that we glimpse the darker and more 'genuine' Doctor. A Doctor who is conscious always that he is essentially homeless, and that he 'walks in eternity' . . .

Sarah Jane Smith

Sarah Jane Smith is an investigative journalist. She first met the Third Doctor while working 'under cover', and was soon caught up in his adventures – whisked off back to the Middle Ages in the TARDIS to battle a stranded Sontaran.

It is Sarah's intelligence, determination, loyalty and conviction that the Doctor comes to value and admire. In his fourth incarnation, he describes her not only as his friend – a rare admission for the Doctor – but as his *best* friend. When they are forced to part company as the Doctor is summoned back to Gallifrey both are saddened by Sarah's departure.

But as we now know, this was not the last time they would meet. Intelligent and determined, Sarah never misses the opportunity for a good story and is not afraid to take risks. Of all the Doctor's companions, Sarah Jane Smith is the one whose exploits and adventures after she left the Doctor have continued to fascinate, enthral, and excite us all.

Harry Sullivan

Seconded from the Royal Navy to become UNIT's Medical Officer, Surgeon Lieutenant Harry Sullivan is called in to care for the Doctor after he regenerates into his fourth incarnation. The task is made more difficult as Harry does not appear to be aware of the Doctor's alien physiognomy and is startled to discover he has two heartbeats.

But in the process of keeping a professional eye on the newly regenerated Doctor, Harry soon comes to appreciate his scientific genius, and the Doctor comes to see Harry as a friend. He even invites Harry to join himself and Sarah for a trip in the TARDIS. For Harry, it's a bizarre but life-changing experience.

But despite his bravado and enthusiasm, Harry can also be inept and naïve. At heart, despite his aspirations, Harry is not really an adventurer. He hints that given the chance he would like to retire to become a General Practitioner somewhere quiet in the country. Certainly, at his first opportunity Harry decides to stay behind on Earth and let the Doctor and Sarah travel on in the TARDIS without him . . .

1

Secret Mission

It was a battlefield.

The ground was churned, scarred, ravaged. Nothing grew there, nothing lived. The twisted, rusting wrecks of innumerable war-machines littered the landscape. There were strands of ragged, tangled wire, collapsed dugouts, caved-in trenches. The perpetual twilight was made darker by fog. Thick, dank and evil, it swirled close to the muddy ground, hiding some of the horrors from view.

Something stirred in the mud. A goggled, helmeted head peered over a ridge, surveyed the shattered landscape. A hand beckoned, and more shapes rose and shambled forwards. There were about a dozen of them, battle-weary men in ragged uniforms, their weapons a strange mixture of old and new, their faces hidden by gas-masks. A star-shell burst over their heads, bathing them for a moment in its sickly green light before it sputtered into darkness. The thump of artillery came from somewhere in the distance, with the hysterical chatter of automatic weapons. But the firing was some distance away. Too tired even to react, the patrol shambled on its way.

A man materialised out of the fog and stood looking in bewilderment after the soldiers. He was a very tall man, dressed in comfortable old tweed trousers and a loosely-hanging jacket. An amazingly long scarf was wound round his neck, a battered, broad-rimmed hat was jammed on to a tangle of curly brown hair. Hands deep in his pockets, he pivoted slowly on his heels, turning in a complete circle to survey the desolate landscape.

He shook his head, the bright blue eyes clouded with puzzlement. This was all wrong, he thought. It was all terribly wrong. The transmat beam should have taken him back to the space station. Instead he was here, in this terrible place. How could it possibly have happened?

'Greetings, Doctor.'

The Doctor spun round at the sound of the voice behind him. A tall, distinguished figure in flowing robes stood looking at him quizzically. A Time Lord! The Doctor knew all about Time Lords—he was one himself. He had left his own people untold years ago to roam through Space and Time in his 'borrowed' TARDIS. He'd rebelled against the Time Lords, been captured and exiled by them, and had at last made his peace with them. He had served them often, sometimes willingly, sometimes not. These days their hold on him was tenuous. But it was still a hold, a limitation of his freedom, and the Doctor never failed to resent it.

He glared at the elegant figure before him. 'So! I've been hijacked!' he said indignantly. 'Don't you realise how dangerous it is to interfere with a transmat beam?'

'Oh come, Doctor! Not with our techniques. We transcended such simple mechanical devices when the Universe was young.' The languid voice held all the effortless superiority that the Doctor always found so infuriating.

He controlled himself with a mighty effort. 'Whatever I may have done, whatever crimes I committed in your eyes, I have made ample restitution. I have done you great services, and I was given my freedom as a reward. I will not tolerate this continual interference in my lives!'

The Time Lord looked thoughtfully at him and began to stroll across the battlefield, with the air of someone taking a turn on the lawn at a garden party. The dull rumble of gunfire came from somewhere in the distance. '*Continual* interference, Doctor? We pride ourselves we seldom intervene in the affairs of others.'

'Except mine,' the Doctor said bitterly. He hurried after the Time Lord.

'Ah, but you are an exception, Doctor—a special case. You enjoy the freedom we allow you. Occasionally, *not* continually, we ask you to do something for us.'

The Doctor came to a halt, his arms folded. 'I won't do it,' he said obstinately. 'Whatever you want—I won't do it!'

The Time Lord spoke one word. 'Daleks.'

The Doctor spun round. 'Daleks? Well, what about them?'

The Time Lord paused, as if collecting his arguments, then said, 'Our latest temporal projections foresee a time-stream in which the Daleks will have destroyed all other life-forms. They could become the dominant creatures in the Universe.'

'That has always been their aim,' agreed the Doctor grimly. 'Go on.'

'We'd like you to return to Skaro at a point in time just *before* the Daleks evolved.'

Immediately the Doctor guessed the Time Lord's plan. 'And prevent their creation?'

'That, or alter their genetic development, so they evolve into less aggressive creatures. At the very least, you might discover some weakness which could serve as a weapon against them.'

The Doctor tried to look as if he was thinking it over. But it was no more than a pretence. He couldn't resist the idea of a chance to defeat his oldest enemies once and for all. 'Oh all right. All right. I suppose I'll have to help you—just one more time. Return me to the TARDIS.'

'No need for that, Doctor. This is Skaro.' The Time Lord gestured at the desolate scene around them.

'Skaro—after a thousand years of war between Kaleds and Thals. We thought it would save time if we assumed your agreement.' He tossed something to the Doctor, who caught it instinctively. He found himself holding a heavy, ornately-designed bangle in a metal that looked something like copper. It wasn't copper, of course, any more than the object was the simple ornament it appeared to be. 'A Time Ring, Doctor. It will return you to the TARDIS when your mission is finished. Don't lose it, will you? It's your life-line. Good luck.' The Time Lord vanished as suddenly and silently as he had appeared.

'Just a minute,' yelled the Doctor. 'What about my two human companions?'

As if in answer a voice called from the fog. 'Doctor? Where are you?'

'Sarah?' The Doctor began running towards the sound. Almost immediately he lost his balance and skidded down a long muddy slope. Sarah Jane Smith and Harry Sullivan were waiting for him at the edge of a big shell crater.

Sarah was a slim, pretty girl in fashionable clothes. On Earth she was a journalist, though that life seemed very far away now. Harry was a square-jawed, blue-eyed, curly-haired young man. He had the rather dated good looks of the hero of an old-fashioned adventure story. Harry was a Naval man, a doctor. He was attached to UNIT, the Security Organisation to which the Doctor was Scientific Adviser. Harry had made the mistake of doubting the power of the TARDIS. This amazing device, in appearance an old-fashioned police box, was in fact the machine in which the Doctor travelled through Time and Space. Harry had rashly accepted the Doctor's challenge to 'come for a little trip'. Now, after a number of terrifying adventures, he often wondered if he would ever see Earth again.

The Doctor's two companions looked at him indignantly. 'I say, that was a pretty rough landing,' protested Harry.

Sarah had known the Doctor for longer than Harry; her travels had accustomed her to rough landings and unexpected destinations.

'All right, Doctor, where are we? This isn't the beacon.' They were supposed to be returning by transmat beam to the space station, where the TARDIS was waiting to carry them home.

The Doctor looked at her apologetically. 'I'm afraid there's been a slight change of plan . . .'

There was a sudden whistling sound. The Doctor wrapped his arms around his two friends and threw himself into the crater, dragging them with him. They raised their heads to protest—then lowered them hurriedly as heavy-artillery shells roared overhead. One thudded into the rim of the crater, showering them with mud.

The barrage went on for an appallingly long time, but at last it died away. The Doctor lifted his head and looked cautiously out of the crater. '*Not* what you'd call a very friendly welcome.'

He turned at a muffled scream from Sarah. She pointed shakily. They were not alone in the crater. A raggedly-uniformed soldier crouched on the other side, his rifle aimed straight at them. Nobody moved. Then the Doctor walked cautiously towards the soldier. The man didn't react. The Doctor touched him on the shoulder and the soldier pitched forward, landing face-down in the mud.

The Doctor knelt beside him. 'It's all right, Sarah, the poor fellow's dead.' The Doctor examined the body, noticing the strangely shaped gas-mask, the holstered hand-blaster, the ancient projectile rifle. He pointed out the last two items to Harry. 'You see? These two weapons are separated by centuries of technology.'

Sarah joined them. She pointed to a small dial sewn into the ragged combat-jacket. 'What's this thing, Doctor?'

'A radiation detector.'

'Worn with a gas-mask straight out of the First World War?' asked Harry incredulously.

Sarah examined the uniform more closely. 'That combat-jacket's some synthetic fibre—and the rest of the uniform seems to be made of animal skins!'

The Doctor nodded. 'It's like finding the remains of a stone-age man with a transistor radio.'

7

Harry chuckled. 'Playing rock music, eh?' Even in the most macabre circumstances, Harry could not resist a joke. He looked at the others, hurt at their lack of reaction. '*Rock* music—cave-man—get it?'

Sarah threw him an impatient look and said, 'What does it all mean, Doctor?'

'A thousand-year war,' the Doctor said sadly. 'A once highly-developed civilisation on the point of total collapse. Come along, you two.'

He jumped out of the crater. Sarah scrambled after him. 'Where are we going?'

'Forward, of course.'

The Doctor set off at a great pace, Sarah and Harry following. They were picking their way through a very nasty clump of barbed wire when the Doctor stopped. His keen eyes had seen a sinister shape, half-buried in the mud.

'What is it?' asked Sarah.

Apologetically the Doctor said, 'I'm afraid we seem to be in the middle of a mine-field. Keep close behind, and follow in my footsteps.'

'You sound just like good King Wenceslas.'

The nightmare journey continued. Fog swirled around them, gunfire rumbled in the distance, and their feet squelched through clammy, clinging mud. In between studying the ground beneath his feet, the Doctor swept occasional glances about the desolate landscape.

'What is it, Doctor? Have you seen something?' asked Harry.

'I'm not sure. I keep getting the feeling we're being watched.'

'Me too,' said Sarah. 'Ever since we set off . . .'

'Rubbish,' said Harry vigorously. 'There's nothing out there except mud and fog.'

'Then let's hope it's just my over-active imagination.' Still looking around him, the Doctor took another step forward. Suddenly he stopped. Beneath the mud, his foot was jammed against something round and metallic. Silently the Doctor pointed downwards. Harry and Sarah looked.

All three held their breath. Slowly the Doctor started to withdraw his foot, then stopped at once as he felt the movement of the mine. He spoke in a quiet, conversational voice. 'Harry, this mine seems to be resting on something solid. If I move my foot it will tilt—and that could be enough to detonate it.'

Harry edged cautiously forward and dropped to his knees beside the half-buried mine. He began clearing mud and gravel away from the mine's surface. The Doctor stood motionless, like someone caught in a game of 'Statues'.

'Seems to be a rock underneath,' said Harry slowly.

Sarah spoke in a whisper, as though the very sound of her voice might be enough to explode the mine.

9

'Can't you wedge it, Harry? Jam something underneath to make it firm?'

Without looking up, Harry said, 'That's what I'm trying to do, old girl.' He groped round the surrounding area and picked up a suitably-sized lump of rock. Very slowly he slipped it between the mine and the rock on which it rested, holding the mine steady with his free hand. 'All right, Doctor, give it a try. Sarah, you back away—and keep to our footsteps.' Sarah obeyed—it was no time to argue.

'You get back as well, Harry,' said the Doctor.

Still crouching at the Doctor's feet, Harry shook his head. 'No. You'll have a better chance if I hold the mine steady while you move.'

'Don't be stupid, Harry.'

'Don't waste time arguing, Doctor. Just move that foot—gently.'

The Doctor moved it. Nothing happened. He watched as Harry Sullivan took first one hand and then the other from the mine. It didn't shift. The Doctor let out a long sigh of relief. 'Thank you, Harry.'

'My pleasure, Doctor,' said Harry Sullivan, a little shakily.

(As they moved clear of the minefield, a huge twisted figure in a shapeless fur hood slipped after them through the fog. The Doctor's and Sarah's instincts had been right. Something was following them across the battlefield . . .)

The Doctor trudged to the top of a long steep rise. He stopped and pointed. 'Look!'

Harry and Sarah joined him. There in the distance they saw—what? A giant, semi-transparent dome, fog swirling around its base, odd shapes just discernible beneath it.

'A protective dome,' said the Doctor softly. 'Large enough to cover an entire city.'

Harry gazed at it in wonder. 'If these people can build something like that, why are they fighting a war with barbed-wire and land-mines?'

'Why indeed,' replied the Doctor.

Sarah looked at him curiously. 'Doctor, isn't it time we had a few explanations?'

The Doctor sighed. 'Yes, of course it is. I must begin with an apology . . .' Briefly the Doctor told them how the Time Lords had intervened to prevent their safe return to the TARDIS, and of the vital mission that had been imposed on him. 'I'm only sorry you two were caught up in their high-handed action.'

He seemed so genuinely distressed that Sarah said, 'That's all right, Doctor. Not your fault is it, Harry?'

'Of course not. If these Daleks are as bad as you say, it'll be a pleasure to help scuttle 'em.'

The Doctor grinned, spirits restored by Harry's cheerful confidence.

'So where do we begin?' asked Sarah, sounding a good deal braver than she actually felt.

The Doctor pointed towards the dome. 'There!' he said. And they started moving towards the distant city.

But *getting* to the city wasn't so easy. It was guarded by an elaborate system of interconnecting trenches, similar to those that had covered Europe during the First World War. Fortunately the trench network appeared to be completely deserted. The Doctor and his companions were going through a kind of maze, moving, they hoped, ever nearer to the mysterious city.

'Maybe all the troops have been withdrawn,' suggested Harry.

'Or killed,' said the Doctor. 'See here.'

They followed him round a corner and found themselves in a large trench, floored with wooden planks and barricaded with sandbags. It was lined with men, propped up along its edge as if awaiting attack. 'Even the dead have a part to play in this war,' said the Doctor. 'They've been stood here to make the trench look fully manned.'

They moved along the row of silent figures. Harry examined one more closely. 'Same scrappy uniform as that chap in the crater. Seems to be different insignia though.'

'Different side, Harry,' the Doctor said. 'He was one of the attackers. These are defending the city.'

Sarah shivered as she glanced at the line of dead men, their sightless eyes staring out into the fog. She wandered further along the trench. Set deep into the rear wall was a heavy metal door. 'Look at this,' she called out.

Harry and the Doctor joined her. 'We must be getting near the city,' said the Doctor. 'That's probably the entrance to some kind of service tunnel.'

Harry heaved on the door, but it wouldn't budge. 'Seems to be locked solid,' he grunted.

Suddenly there was a whistling sound, followed by a thud from over the rim of the trench. Cautiously the Doctor looked out. A metal projectile lay half-buried in the mud. Evil-looking green smoke was welling out of it, and creeping slowly towards the trench.

The Doctor jumped back. 'Look out,' he yelled. 'Poison gas, and it's coming this way!'

2

Prisoners of War

The Doctor was already reaching for one of the propped-up bodies. 'Get gas-masks, quickly!' he shouted. Sarah and Harry ran to obey.

It wasn't particularly pleasant grappling with the stiff, cold corpses, but things were too desperate for any fastidiousness. All three pulled tight the straps of their gas-masks, just as green smoke began creeping into the trench.

There was a sudden burst of rifle fire. Bullets sprayed the edge of the trench, thudding into the sandbags and whining over their heads.

The Doctor peered cautiously out. A small group of ragged soldiers was pelting towards them, yelling and firing as they came. He turned to shout a warning to Sarah and Harry, but it was already too late. Troops leapt over the sandbags and dropped into the trench. Seeing the gas-masked forms of the Doctor and his companions, they hurled themselves upon them.

They had no chance to explain their neutrality. Within minutes they were engaged in savage hand-to-hand fighting. Luckily the trench was so packed with struggling bodies that the attackers had no chance to use their weapons, not daring to shoot for fear of hitting each other. The Doctor and Harry closed ranks to defend Sarah. They put up a splendid fight. Harry had boxed for the Navy in his time and he dealt out straight rights, lefts and uppercuts in the best traditions of the boxing ring. The Doctor fought in a whirl of long arms and legs, using the techniques of Venusian Aikido to drop one opponent after another. But so heavily were the two outnumbered that the sheer weight of bodies soon bore them down.

Crouched in one corner of the trench, Sarah heard a grinding noise. Peering through the struggling mass of bodies, she saw the heavy metal door slide open. A fresh contingent of soldiers appeared. They were better uniformed than the first attackers, and better armed too. There was a sudden fierce chattering of automatic weapons. Sarah jumped up to warn the Doctor, but a wild swing from a rifle-butt caught her on the temple. She collapsed face downwards.

The Doctor heard the chatter of machine-guns and realised that the character of the battle had changed. These new arrivals had no hesitation in shooting. 'Down, Harry!' he yelled, and flung himself to the ground. As the two dropped down, heavy shapes began falling on top of them—the now bullet-ridden corpses of their first attackers.

Shielded by the bodies of their former opponents, the Doctor and Harry laid low.

The rattle of machine-gun fire ended at last. The leader of the victorious soldiers saw that the green gas had drifted away. He pulled the gas-mask from his face and took in great gulps of the foggy air. He was very young. As the others pulled off their gas-masks it could be seen that they too were little more than boys.

Pushing aside the dead body which held him down, Harry began struggling to his feet. Instantly the nearest soldier raised his gun. The Doctor struggled up, shouting, 'No . . .'

Then came the sound of more shooting from outside the trench, the yelling of a fresh wave of attackers. The leader indicated the Doctor and Harry. 'Into the tunnel with them—quick!' Harry and the Doctor were clubbed down and dragged unconscious through the metal door. The leader followed his men, and the door clanged shut behind them.

Outside the trench the sounds of yelling and shooting faded as the attack moved on to another section of the line. Hidden beneath a pile of bodies, Sarah lay unconscious, a trickle of blood running from her temple.

Harry and the Doctor were carried along a dark tunnel into a small, concrete-walled room at its far end. The place was primitively furnished with wooden tables, benches and a couple of bunks. One of the tables held some kind of field communications equipment. On the far side of the room was an arched opening in which stood a small passenger trolley. The trolley was on rails which disappeared into the blackness of the tunnel. It looked like the terminus of a miniature underground railway.

As the patrol crowded into the room, Harry and the Doctor were dumped casually on the ground. The soldiers began struggling out of their equipment.

Looking at his two prisoners with a satisfied air, the young patrol leader wrenched the gas-masks from their faces. His expression changed to one of puzzlement. 'They don't *look* like Thals . . .' He thought for a moment. 'Stick them in the transporter, I'll take them to Command Headquarters.' A couple of soldiers grabbed the two prisoners and threw them into the trolley. The patrol leader climbed in after them and operated controls. The trolley rumbled away into the darkness.

Harry and the Doctor recovered to find themselves rattling through pitch darkness at terrifying speed. The trolley shot into a big, well-lighted area and jolted to a halt. Armed guards swarmed round and dragged them along more concrete corridors and into a large room.

By now the Doctor had recovered enough to take an interest in his surroundings. They were in some kind of central command post. Maps covered the walls, there was more communications equipment, and in the centre of the room was a huge map table holding a relief map, a kind of model landscape. It seemed to depict *two* dome-covered cities, with the trench-riddled battle-field between them. A fitting image for the present state of Skaro, thought the Doctor. He noticed that the guards were smartly uniformed here, their weapons modern and well cared for. Strange how all wars were the same, thought the Doctor. The staff back at H.Q. always had better conditions than the men actually out fighting . . .

A tall, very young officer, elegant in his gold-braided uniform, was shifting symbols on the relief map. He straightened up and looked coldly at the patrol leader. 'Well?'

'Two prisoners, General Ravon. Captured in section one-zero-one. For interrogation.'

The officer smiled. 'Excellent. I enjoy interrogations.'

The Doctor looked at him. The young face was hard and cold. 'Yes,' he said cheerfully, 'I must say, you look the type.'

A blow from the rifle-butt of one of the guards sent the Doctor staggering. 'Insolent muto,' said Ravon. He turned to the patrol leader who stood rigidly to attention, obviously waiting to speak. 'Well, what is it?'

'My section totally destroyed the Thal attackers, sir, except for these two prisoners. But—well, the men are exhausted, and ammunition is running low.'

'Your men will fight until they are relieved. As for ammunition, conserve it. Use the spears and knives you were issued with whenever possible. Return to your patrol.'

'Sir.' The patrol leader saluted wearily and marched out, taking the guards with him. The Doctor glanced quickly round the room. Except for the soldier manning the communications unit, they were now alone with the General . . .

As if guessing the Doctor's thoughts, Ravon drew his blaster and covered the two prisoners. 'So—the Thals have degenerated to recruiting mutos, have they? Turn out your pockets!'

The Doctor shrugged. 'Why not? I always try to turn them out every year or so!' He began piling up an incredible assortment of junk on the edge of the map table—a yo-yo, a bag of jelly babies, several lengths of string and a miscellaneous collection of scientific instruments. As he did so, he took the opportunity to study the relief map.

Ravon noticed the Doctor's interest.

'Take a good look,' he sneered. 'In a few weeks we're going to change the shape of that map for ever. We shall sweep the Thals from the face of Skaro!' A note of hysteria was in his voice.

The Doctor studied him thoughtfully. Basic insecurity there—or why would he bother to boast to a couple of prisoners. In tones of deliberate provocation the Doctor said, 'Oh yes? And how are you going to do that—with worn-out soldiers, no ammunition and boy generals?'

Ravon reacted with hysterical rage. 'You've been warned about your insolence——'

Harry Sullivan, who had been watching all this with keen if baffled interest, felt a pressure from the Doctor's foot on his own. He tensed, ready for the next move.

The Doctor gave Ravon one of his sudden, brilliant smiles. 'I'm sorry, General. But you do seem to be having problems with this final campaign.'

Ravon felt he had to convince this infuriating prisoner. 'When victory is ours, we shall wipe every trace of the Thals and their city from this planet. We will avenge the deaths of all the Kaleds who have fallen. Our battlecry will be, "Total extermination of the Thals".' Ravon's voice had risen to a ritual chant. He was repeating a lesson drummed into him since childhood. Deliberately the Doctor made his own voice low and soothing.

'That's very impressive, General. You mean you're going to *sweep* across these trenches . . .' The Doctor suited his actions to his words, flinging one arm out in a sweeping gesture. At the end of it, the edge of his hand hit Ravon's wrist in a precisely timed blow. Ravon's hand opened, the blaster flew through the air. Harry Sullivan caught it with the skill of a born cricketer. The Doctor turned to Ravon, who was rubbing his hand. 'Did I hurt your fingers, old chap?'

The soldier at the communications set turned round to find Harry covering him with the blaster.

'You won't get out of here alive,' Ravon blustered feebly. The Doctor ignored him. He crossed to the communications set, took the blaster from the startled soldier and put the set out of action with a few well-aimed blows. Outraged, the soldier jumped him—and the Doctor silenced him with a swift tap from the blaster. He lowered him gently to the floor with genuine regret.

The Doctor's expression hardened as he swung back to Ravon. 'Now then, Alexander the Great, you're going to take us out of here.'

Ravon struck a heroic attitude. 'Never!'

Harry jammed the blaster under his chin. 'You won't get any medals for being stupid, General. In fact you won't get any more medals for anything—ever.'

Ravon looked from the Doctor to Harry. These two ruffians were obviously desperate men. Surely his own life was too valuable to risk? It wasn't as if they stood any real chance of escaping . . .

'All right. Where do you want me to take you?'

'Back to where we were captured,' said the Doctor. 'We left a friend behind.'

'In the Wastelands?' said Ravon. 'Yes, I suppose that's home to you mutos, isn't it? Well, come on. I can promise you won't get far.'

The Doctor and Harry fell into step beside Ravon, the stolen blasters concealed in their pockets. Ravon led

22

them out of the room and along the corridor. Passing guards glanced curiously at them, but no one dared question the actions of the General.

They followed him along one corridor after another, twisting and turning until Harry at least had lost all sense of direction. He gave Ravon a jab. 'Where are you taking us? This isn't the way we came.'

'There's a platform lift at the end of this tunnel. You know what a lift is, don't you, muto?'

'Yes, but I don't know what a muto is,' said Harry. 'You're making a mistake, General.'

'If you come from the Wastelands, you're mutos!' Clearly that settled the matter for Ravon, and Harry didn't bother to argue. The lift appeared at the end of the corridor. Ravon touched a control beside it, and they all stood waiting.

Harry gave the Doctor a worried look. 'I hope Sarah's still there.'

Ravon couldn't resist the opportunity to sneer.

'If you're *not* mutos, then you won't last long up there.'

There came the sound of jackbooted feet on the concrete floor. Someone was walking along the corridor towards them. Harry gave Ravon a warning jab with the hidden blaster in his pocket. 'Just remember we're your friends, won't you?'

The newcomer was a slightly built, thin-faced man. His black uniform was plain except for silver insignia, and seemed somehow different from Ravon's. Not a soldier, thought the Doctor, but some kind of policeman. Ravon's greeting confirmed the Doctor's theory. 'Greetings, Security-Commander Nyder.'

Nyder's reply was equally formal. 'Greetings, General Ravon. I was just on my way to see you.' He stared curiously at the oddly assorted trio. The Doctor beamed, and Harry managed a curt nod. Nasty-looking customer, he thought.

Ravon coughed nervously. 'Perhaps you would be kind enough to go to my office and wait. I shall only be a few minutes longer.'

Nyder nodded, but made no attempt to move on. He looked more closely at the Doctor and Harry. 'You're civilians?'

The Doctor nodded. 'Just here on a brief visit to our old friend General Ravon. Don't let us detain you.'

'You won't.' As if satisfied with this riposte, Nyder started to walk away. Then suddenly he jumped back, drawing a pistol. 'Ravon—get down!' he shouted.

Ravon flung himself to the ground as Nyder fired at the Doctor. The bullet sang past his head, chipping concrete fragments from the wall. The Doctor yelled, 'Run for it, Harry,' and the two fugitives disappeared round the corner.

Nyder produced a pocket communicator. 'Alert all guards. Two Thal intruders in command complex. Sound the alarm.'

A few seconds later, a high-pitched siren began to blare through the corridors. Nyder looked at Ravon, who was shamefacedly picking himself up. 'You're a fool, General Ravon,' he said dispassionately.

Ravon tried to justify himself. 'They took me by surprise.'

'What kind of soldier allows two unarmed prisoners to overpower him in his own headquarters?'

Stung by Nyder's scorn, Ravon said, 'Those weren't ordinary prisoners. There's something different about them. They're not mutos and they're not Thals.'

Nyder looked at him sceptically. 'No? Well, if they *are different*—we'll find out when they're recaptured.' There was total confidence in his voice.

The Doctor and Harry sprinted along a corridor with no idea where they were going. Their one thought was to escape the pursuing guards. Unfortunately more guards appeared ahead, and only a providential side-corridor saved them from capture. Shots ringing all round them they turned left, then right, ran down an even smaller corridor and found themselves in a dead end. The corridor ended in a pair of lift doors like the ones where they'd left Ravon and Nyder. They turned to go back, but heard guards running towards them. Instinctively the Doctor pressed the lift controls. The running feet came nearer. As guards appeared in the corridor the lift doors opened and Harry and the Doctor dived inside. The soldiers raised their guns, the Doctor stabbed frantically at the controls, and the lift doors closed—just in time to save Harry and the Doctor from a hail of bullets.

Nyder arrived to see what had happened. He snatched out his communicator. 'Alert surface patrols to watch for intruders in lift area seven!'

The high-speed lift whisked Harry and the Doctor to the surface in a matter of seconds. The doors opened on a featureless stretch of open country—Wasteland as Ravon had called it. As yet no soldiers were in sight. Harry stared out into the drifting fog. 'Where to, Doctor?'

Figures loomed out of the fog, then came the sound of shouted orders. 'Just keep running,' called the Doctor, and shot off across the battlefield like an ostrich, Harry close behind. The Kaled patrol lumbered after them.

The Doctor and Harry tore across the churned-up landscape leaping over pill-boxes, dodging barbed-wire, stumbling in and out of shell holes. In their frantic burst of speed they left the patrol far behind. It began to look as if they had succeeded in making their escape. But the battlefield held more dangers than pursuing soldiers. Stumbling down a muddy slope the Doctor's foot caught some kind of buried trip-wire. He gave Harry a tremendous shove, yelling 'Mine!' and threw himself in the mud beside him. There was a muffled 'crump', and a fountain of mud shot up in the air as the long-buried mine was detonated. Harry and the

Doctor escaped the flying shrapnel but they were close enough to be deafened and half-stunned by the blast.

Dizzily they stumbled to their feet, shaking their heads to clear the ringing in their ears. The Doctor rubbed the mud from his eyes and glanced round.

They were completely surrounded by the Kaled patrol, covered by a ring of rifles. The Doctor looked round at the circle of hostile faces. Slowly he raised his hands. Now what was it they said on Earth, back in the Kaiser's day?

The Doctor smiled round at the soldiers. 'Kamerade?' he said hopefully. No one smiled back. The soldiers began to close in.

3

The Secret Weapon

The Doctor and Harry were marched across the Wastelands, into the lift, through the corridors of the Command Centre and back into the room they had just left. Security-Commander Nyder and General Ravon were waiting for them. Nyder was turning over the odds and ends taken from the Doctor's pockets. He held up a small, complex instrument surmounted with a dial. 'What is the function of this object?'

The Doctor leaned forward and examined it. 'Very interesting little gadget, that,' he said chattily. 'Actually it's an etheric beam locator—but you *can* use it for detecting ion-charged emissions.'

Clearly Nyder was none the wiser. 'It is not of Thal manufacture.'

'Well, of course not. My friend and I don't come from your planet.'

Nyder turned the instrument over in his hands. 'I have heard Davros say there is no intelligent life on other planets. And Davros is never wrong—about anything.'

'Then he must be an exceptional man. Even I am occasionally wrong about *some* things. Who is Davros?'

Nyder looked at the Doctor keenly, then realised that the question was genuine. 'Davros is our greatest scientist. He is in charge of all scientific research in the Bunker.'

Ravon, who had been standing by in the background, made an attempt to assert himself. 'They could be mutos, Commander Nyder. Mutos who've managed to develop some kind of technology . . .'

Nyder gave him a look of silent contempt, but said nothing. Harry, equally silent up to now, burst out, 'Look here, I wish you wouldn't keep calling us mutos. We don't even know what they are.'

Nyder looked wonderingly at him. 'Mutos are scarred and twisted monsters created by the chemical and radiation weapons used in the early part of this war. They were banished to the Wastelands, where they scavenge like the animals they have become.'

'In other words, you just abandon your genetic wounded?' There was horror in the Doctor's voice.

'The Kaled race *must* be kept pure. The imperfect are rejected, sent into the Wastelands. Some of them survive.'

'That's a very harsh policy.'

Nyder shifted uncomfortably. 'Your views are unimportant,' he said dismissively. 'General Ravon—I am taking these two prisoners for interrogation by the Special Unit.'

'But they are prisoners of the Army . . .'

'You will release them to me. The Special Unit will get more out of them than your crude methods.'

Ravon crumpled before the cold authority in Nyder's voice. 'If you insist . . .'

'I do insist.' Nyder produced a sheaf of papers from inside his tunic. 'I have a list of supply requirements here. All these items are to be delivered to the Bunker immediately.'

Ravon scanned the list with growing resentment. 'I simply cannot spare this amount of equipment. Your spare-parts requisition alone would take over half my available supply.'

Nyder smiled coldly. 'General Ravon, you will notice that the requisitions are counter-signed by Davros himself. Perhaps you would prefer to discuss the matter with him?'

Ravon shuddered, and shook his head. 'I'll have the supplies at the Bunker by dawn.'

'By midnight, General. The orders specify midnight.'

'Very well. Midnight.'

Nyder turned to the guards. 'Bring the prisoners.'

As they were marched away after him, the Doctor thought that it had been a very interesting demonstration. It was clear that the real power among the Kaleds lay not with the army, but with Davros, and those who served him.

*

Sarah had one of the most horrifying awakenings of her life. Buried beneath a pile of rapidly stiffening corpses, she could feel her face wet with blood. At first she felt confusedly that she must be dead too, or at least badly wounded. But as she struggled groggily to her feet she realised that the blood came from a shallow cut on her forehead. Miraculously, she was more or less unharmed.

She looked around. Along the line of the trench lay still more bodies, sprawled in the grotesque and ungainly attitudes of sudden death. The metal door was closed. There was no sign of the Doctor or Harry. Sarah began to move along the trench calling softly, 'Doctor? Doctor, are you there? Harry?' There was no answer. She paused, thinking. It would do her no good to stay here. She started to climb out of the trench.

Sarah wandered across the Wastelands for what seemed a very long time, with no clear idea of where she was going or why. The grey half-light, combined with the drifting fog, made visibility very low. She stumbled in and out of shell holes, and disentangled herself from clumps of rusting barbed wire. Occasionally she heard distant gunfire, but saw no soldiers. Clearly the battle had moved away from this section of the line. All the time she had a feeling of something following her, of unseen forms creeping towards her. It was this, as much as any real hope of finding the Doctor, that kept her staggering wearily on her way.

As the darkness deepened, the following shapes moved closer. Sarah told herself it was all imagination, but she knew very well it was not. At last she paused exhausted, and a hideous shapeless *something* loomed out of the darkness, reaching for her. Sarah screamed and ran. The shapeless thing pursued her and soon others joined in the chase. She was hunted across the Wastelands, soft footsteps thudding behind her. Fear gave her fresh energy and she ran blindly at full speed, taking no care where she was going. Suddenly the ground vanished beneath her feet . . . She felt herself falling. It wasn't a long fall, something like five or six feet, and luckily she landed on soft ground. But it was enough to knock the breath out of her. She lay gasping, pressed close to the ground, and to her relief heard the sounds of pursuit pass by.

Scrambling to her feet, Sarah began to take a look at her surroundings. Close by she could just distinguish the outline of a broken wall. She moved towards it and felt her way along. It seemed she had fallen into the basement of a ruined house. She decided she might as well stay. At least the ruins offered a chance of rest and safety. She made her way out of the basement, climbing some broken steps. As she reached the top, Sarah suddenly drew back. She was in a ruined entrance hall. She could see the sky through the broken roof. Light was streaming from a room on the other side of the hall. Sarah crept up cautiously, feeling that she was more likely to meet enemies than friends on this dreadful planet.

Flattening herself against the wall, she peeped into the room. It was a large room, and might once have been some kind of conference chamber. A space had been cleared in the centre of the rubble littered floor, and a portable field-lamp made a central pool of light. On the far edge of the cleared area, a man was setting up a target, a life-sized, wooden cut-out in the shape of a soldier. The man wore the white coat of a scientist. He was tall and thin, and his features had the dark, thin-faced intense look, so typical of most Kaleds.

There was another man in the room, but Sarah was unable to see him clearly. He was on the near side of the pool of light, his back to her, and was almost hidden by shadows. All Sarah could see was the back of an elaborate wheelchair. A withered right hand hovered constantly over the controls built into the chair arm.

The man finished setting up the target. 'I am ready, Davros.' He walked over to stand beside the man in the chair, his back to Sarah.

'Observe the test closely, Gharman, my friend. This will be a moment to live in history.' The voice was almost inhuman, filtered through some mechanical reproduction system. It had a harsh, grating quality that Sarah found familiar. She saw the claw-like hand touch a switch. There was a whirring sound from the outer darkness and something moved into the pool of light. It was a gleaming metal creature with a rounded base. The body was constructed of heavily-studded metal panels, the top was a dome from which projected a lens on a metal stalk. Sarah recognised the creature at once. It was a Dalek.

True, it wasn't a fully-evolved Dalek, the kind she had seen in ruthless action on the planet of the Exxilons. The movements were jerky and the arm with the curious sucker-like tip was missing. But the gun was there, and the eye-stalk . . . This must be an early model, a kind of prototype. Sarah realised that the calculations of the Time Lords had been accurate. The Doctor and his friends had been brought to Skaro as the Daleks were about to be born.

Davros was putting the Dalek through its paces. 'Left, left, forward . . . now right. Stop.' The Dalek obeyed, its movements faltering and uncertain. Sarah realised now why the voice of Davros had sounded so familiar. It was just like that of the Dalek he had created!

At last Davros had the Dalek position to his satisfaction. It stood in front of his chair, opposite the target on the other side of the room. 'Now,' grated Davros. 'EXTERMINATE!'

The Dalek's gun roared, and the target exploded in flames.

'Excellent,' said Davros. 'Locomotion is still faulty, and we must improve the sense-organs. But the weaponry is perfect. We can begin!'

As Davros's chair swivelled round Sarah jumped back into hiding. Crouched low she saw the shape in the chair glide past her, followed by the Dalek. Gharman came last, carrying the field-lamp. Sarah watched the bobbing light move away across the Wastelands.

She leant against the wall, thinking hard. Obviously she had stumbled on some kind of secret test, and she ought to get the information to the Doctor. But where to look for him? Presumably in the city. Sarah decided to follow Davros. As she started to get up, a huge, misshapen hand reached out of the darkness and touched her lightly on the shoulder. Sarah turned to see the black bulk of a hooded creature looming over her. The shock was too much, and she fainted dead away.

To their surprise, the Doctor and Harry were marched out of the domed city and across several miles of Wasteland. Soon they saw lights ahead, and the shape of a small, low-lying building, a kind of blockhouse. Nyder halted the party by a massive metal door. A voice spoke from a metal grille. 'You will announce your name, rank, serial number, purpose of visit and authorisation reference.'

Nyder glared irritably into what the Doctor guessed must be a hidden camera. 'All right, Tane, use your eyes. This is Security-Commander Nyder with prisoners and escort.'

'Yes, sir,' squawked the voice in evident alarm. Nyder was obviously a character to be feared. The heavy door slid open and they marched through.

They found themselves in a largish ante-room. One wall was filled with complex scientific equipment, and another metal door faced them. Two black-clad officers stood waiting stiffly to attention, one beside the door, the other at a kind of control console. More black-clad guards lined the walls.

Nyder nodded to the first officer. 'Captain Tane, I want these two screened and passed to Ronson. Full interrogation. Here are their belongings.' Handing over a sealed plastic envelope, Nyder turned. The second officer hurriedly touched a control. The inner door opened, revealing a tunnel stretching downwards. Nyder disappeared along it, and the door closed after him. The Doctor gave Harry a reassuring grin. Any situation that started with Nyder leaving couldn't be all bad! He nodded affably to Tane.

'That's a relief. Any chance of a cup of tea?' Tane glared at him speechlessly. 'Any light refreshment would do,' the Doctor added helpfully. 'We've been through some very trying experiences, haven't we, Harry?'

'Very trying, Doctor.' Harry's agreement was heartfelt.

Tane pointed to a sort of upright coffin surrounded with complex instruments. 'Step into the security scan.'

The Doctor glanced at Harry. 'No tea,' he said sadly.

Tane's voice was coldly angry. 'Let me point out to you that you have no rights here. I have full authority to execute any prisoner who does not obey orders.'

Two soldiers seized Harry and shoved him into the scanning device. As soon as he was inside a powerful light shone from above, seeming to pin him down. Harry went rigid, white lights flashed and instruments buzzed all round him.

The lights went out, and Harry staggered out of the machine on the point of collapse. A soldier grabbed him, propped him against the nearest wall, then pushed the Doctor into the machine. Once again the light flashed and the instruments buzzed. But this time there was a new noise; a high-pitched, warning shriek. Tane glanced at the instrument panel. 'Scan detects power-source on prisoner's left wrist.' The scan was concluded, the machine switched off and the Doctor stepped out. At a nod from Tane two guards grabbed him. 'Remove object on the left wrist of the prisoner.' One of the guards started to wrench away the bangle.

The Doctor struggled wildly. 'You can't have that. It isn't a weapon, and it's of no possible interest to you . . .'

A brutal blow from the rifle-butt of one of the guards choked off his protest. Tane took the bracelet, then dropped it into the plastic envelope with the Doctor's other odds and ends. The officer in charge of the scanner gave Tane a sheaf of cards, and he put them in the envelope without looking at them.

As he caught hold of the collapsing Doctor, Harry hissed in his ear, 'Stop making a fuss, Doctor.'

'That Time Bracelet is our only hope of getting back to the TARDIS. We've *got* to get it back.'

'I know that,' whispered Harry. 'But we don't want *them* to know, do we?' The Doctor subsided.

Tane turned to the nearest guard. 'These prisoners are to be given over to the custody of Senior Researcher Ronson. Take this with you.' He handed over the plastic envelope.

The two prisoners were taken through the inner door and down the long tunnel. They were led along endless buttressed corridors and into an enormous underground room. Looking around in interest, the Doctor guessed he was in an advanced research laboratory. Or rather a collection of laboratories. The place was sectioned off, and in different cubicles and enclosed areas white-coated scientists were hard at work. They were taken across the room to a corner desk, where a haggard, grey-haired man sat wearily studying some figures. The guards handed over the envelope and the prisoners, then marched away.

Harry and the Doctor stood waiting before the desk. The grey-haired man tipped out the contents of the envelope and examined them. The Doctor's eyes gleamed at the sight of the Time Bracelet and he took a pace forwards, but Harry nudged him, looking round significantly. The huge room had many doors, but armed guards stood at every one.

The man behind the desk looked up. 'My name is Ronson,' he said. 'Do sit down.' Harry and the Doctor, taken aback by the first kind words they'd heard on Skaro, pulled over a couple of metal chairs and sank into them gratefully.

'Thank you. I take it you're not with the military?' the Doctor asked hopefully.

'I am a member of the Special Scientific Division.'

'Excellent. Perhaps we can have a conversation that isn't punctuated by rifle-butts.' The Doctor rubbed his aching back.

A little shamefacedly Ronson said, 'That depends. If you don't answer my questions satisfactorily, I must hand you back to the Security Guards.' As if glad to leave a distasteful subject, he turned to the objects on his desk. 'Where did you get these things?'

The Doctor smiled. 'Oh, here and there. Different places, different times.'

'If I didn't know better,' said Ronson slowly, 'I would swear they were produced on some other planet. But it's an established scientific fact that Skaro is the only planet capable of supporting life.'

'Suppose there are more planets than you're aware of?' suggested the Doctor gently.

Ronson picked up the batch of coded cards. 'When you went through the scanner the instruments checked your physical make-up—encephalographical patterns, physiological composition and so on. So if you are from another world . . .' His voice faded away as he studied the cards.

'You were saying?' asked the Doctor politely.

Ronson looked up with awe in his eyes. '*His* make-up,' he nodded towards Harry, 'is comparable to ours, with a few minor differences. But yours . . . Nothing conforms to any known life-form on this planet. *Nothing*—except the external appearance.'

'Just goes to show—you should never judge by appearances.'

Ronson leaned forward. 'Who are you? Where do you come from? Tell me.' The Doctor recognised pure scientific curiosity in Ronson's voice.

'It's a very long story. Do you have any knowledge of the Theory of Space Dimension Co-related to Relative Time?'

The Doctor was interrupted by a low gonging sound. Every single scientist, Ronson included, reacted with eager attention. The sound stopped and a voice said, 'Davros will address the Elite Scientific Corps in the main laboratory assembly.' Almost at once more white-coated scientists began to enter the room, workers from the adjoining laboratories.

'Our session will have to wait,' Ronson said. 'Davros is coming.' His voice was hushed with reverence.

'I gather Davros is your Chief Scientist?'

'Our Chief Scientist and our supreme commander. He must have something of importance to tell us.'

'I shall be interested to meet him,' said the Doctor politely. But even he was not prepared for the strange apparition that glided into the room. The Doctor was seeing, at close range and in clear lighting, the strange being Sarah had only glimpsed during the secret test in the ruined building.

Davros was no more than the shattered, ruined remnant of what had once been a man. He glided along in an advanced form of wheelchair that moved under its own power. The withered husk of a body was swathed in a high-collared, green plastic overall, and surrounded by a variety of life-support systems. The Doctor guessed that both heart and lungs were mechanically operated and maintained. Only the right hand was visible, a withered claw hovering constantly over the controls built into one arm of the chair. But the most horrifying thing about Davros was his face. Parchment-thin skin clung to the outlines of the shrivelled skull. The eye-sockets were blank and sunken, the mouth a lipless slit. A helmet-like arrangement of wires and plastic tubes surmounted the head, supporting a single lens that rested in the centre of the forehead. Speech, sight and hearing must be mechanically aided too, thought the Doctor.

Harry Sullivan looked at Davros in horror. 'What happened to the poor devil?'

'An atomic shell struck his laboratory during a Thal bombardment,' whispered Ronson. 'His body was shattered, but he *refused* to die. He clung to life, and himself designed the mobile life-support system in which you see him.'

Harry said nothing. To himself he thought that death would surely be preferable to the kind of existence Davros must be leading now.

Davros had taken up his position in the centre of the far wall, flanked by the black-clad figure of Security-Commander Nyder. Davros spoke. 'If I may have your attention . . .' There was utter and complete silence. Helpless in his chair, Davros should have been pitiful. Instead, he was terrifying. The Doctor could almost feel the burning intelligence, the powerful, inflexible will that radiated from the crippled form. 'For some time,' Davros continued, 'I have been busy on a top secret project. There is still much to be done. However, I am anxious that you should see the remarkable progress made so far, and to that end I have arranged this demonstration.' Davros wheeled his chair to face the door by which he had entered. His withered hand dropped to touch a control, and seconds later a metallic shape glided into the room. Like Sarah before him, the Doctor had no difficulty in recognising a Dalek. Armless, weaponless, but still unmistakably a Dalek.

As the machine glided up to Davros, his metallic voice commanded, 'Halt.' The Dalek stopped.

'He's perfected voice-control,' breathed Ronson. 'That's magnificent.'

'Move left. Halt. Move forward. Halt. Circle. Halt.' Obedient to Davros's commands the Dalek moved jerkily about the room.

'Nyder!' The Security-Commander stepped forward. He took a sucker arm and a gun, and fitted them on to the Dalek. 'As you see,' grated Davros, 'our machine is now fitted with a tactile organ and a means of self-defence. I shall turn the machine over to total self-control. It will then be independent of all outside influence. A living, thinking, self-supporting creature.'

Davros touched a switch. For a moment the Dalek did nothing. Then, slowly and uncertainly, it began to move around the room. Davros followed in his wheelchair. Somehow the two were curiously alike. Suddenly the Dalek seemed to see the Doctor. It moved slowly towards his corner, halting just in front of him. The Doctor stood quite still.

'Alien,' croaked the Dalek suddenly. 'Exterminate . . . exterminate . . . exterminate!' Slowly the gun stick raised until it was pointing straight at the Doctor.

4

Rocket of Doom

Nobody moved. It was clear to everyone in the room that the Dalek intended to kill the Doctor. Suddenly Ronson darted forward and flicked one of the switches on Davros's console. Immediately the Dalek 'switched off', gun arm and eye-stalk drooping.

Davros was furious. 'You dare to interfere! You have the audacity to interrupt my experiment!'

Ronson was clearly terrified but he made himself speak out. 'It was going to destroy him.'

'And you consider his worthless life more important than the progress we have made? My creature showed a natural instinct to destroy everything alien—and you interceded.'

'Davros . . . I'm sorry,' pleaded Ronson. 'But this is no ordinary prisoner. I believe he has invaluable information. Let me interrogate him first—then your creature can do what it likes with him.'

Davros considered. 'Very well. You will be punished later for your insubordination. Meanwhile you may interrogate your prisoner until the end of this work-period. After that, I shall resume my experiment.'

Davros wheeled and glided away. Ronson heaved a sigh of relief. The Doctor took a deep breath. 'Thank you,' he said simply.

Ronson seemed hardly able to believe his own temerity. 'I was simply doing my duty. Now you must co-operate with me. If you don't provide knowledge to justify what I have done, Davros will resume his experiment as threatened.'

Nyder crossed over to them. 'Take the prisoners to the cells. You can finish the questioning there. Davros wants them kept safely.'

As the guards bustled them away, the Doctor glanced longingly behind him. The Time Ring still lay among the odds and ends on Ronson's desk . . .

Sarah's faint lasted only a few minutes. She awoke furious with herself—she'd always believed she was the sort of girl who never fainted. As consciousness returned, she heard low whispering voices. She decided to fake unconsciousness a little longer. Two cloaked and hooded figures were crouched beside her, one huge and massive, one thin and spindly. The big one touched her cheek with a misshapen hand. Sarah lay perfectly still. When the figure spoke, its voice was deep and gentle. 'She is beautiful . . . no deformities or imperfections.'

The smaller figure had a shrill whining voice. 'She is a norm, Sevrin. All norms are our enemies. Kill her.'

'Why?' asked the deep voice sadly. 'Why must we always destroy beauty, kill another creature because it is different?'

'Kill her,' the other voice insisted. 'It is the law. All norms must die. If you will not kill her, I will.' The creature produced a knife from under its cloak and long, incredibly thin arms snaked out towards Sarah.

Sevrin moved protectively in front of her, grabbing the knife-wrist. For a moment the two creatures struggled. They broke apart as they heard footsteps and muffled voices. 'A patrol,' muttered Sevrin. 'They're sure to check the building.'

The smaller creature squeaked in panic. 'We must get away.'

'No,' said the deep voice authoritatively. 'Keep still. If you move they'll see you.'

But the slighter figure was already on the move, scuttling spider-like along the wall. From the darkness a voice yelled, 'Halt!'

The glare of a spotlight pinned the shuffling figure. 'Don't move,' ordered the voice, and the sound of booted feet came closer. Suddenly the spindly creature made a run for it. A single shot rang out and it dropped to the ground. Two fair-haired Thal soldiers came forward, one carrying a hand-beam, the other an old-fashioned single-shot rifle. The first shone his light on their kill. 'Only a muto. You wasted your ammunition.'

The soldier with the rifle began to reload. His companion swept the torch-beam along the wall. 'Here, there's a couple more of 'em.'

The torch-beam lit up Sevrin crouching over Sarah's body. The soldier with the rifle took aim, but the other stopped him. 'Hold it. Remember orders. They need expendable labour for the rocket loading.' He shone the torch on Sevrin, pulling the mutant to his feet. 'This one's not so bad. Got all it needs to walk and carry.' Sevrin stood meekly, making no attempt to resist. The soldier shone the lamp down on Sarah. 'No reason this one can't work. Looks almost a norm.' He poked her in the ribs with his foot. 'Come on you, up you get.'

Sarah got slowly to her feet. So much had happened since she'd come to that she was still confused. She staggered a little as she stood up. The soldier with the rifle called, 'No good, this one's too weak and slow. Better let me finish it off.' He raised his rifle.

Sevrin stepped in front of Sarah, shielding her. 'She'll be all right, I promise. I'll help her.'

The soldier hesitated, then nodded. 'All right. Then move.' He gestured with the rifle. Sarah stumbled into the darkness, Sevrin supporting her.

She felt better once she was moving, and was soon able to walk unaided. The soldiers herded them across the Wastelands for what seemed a very long way, until at last they came to within sight of a huge dome-covered city. It was very like the one Sarah had seen earlier with the Doctor and Harry, though the design was slightly different. She nudged Sevrin. 'Where's that?'

He looked at her in surprise. 'It is the city of the Thals.'

They were taken through a guarded access tunnel, along endless concrete corridors, and herded into a huge, bare cell. Small groups of prisoners like themselves were scattered all over the room. Most were cloaked and hooded like Sevrin—mutos, as the soldiers had called them. But there was also a sprinkling of raggedly-uniformed, dark-haired Kaled soldiers. Sarah supposed they must be prisoners of war.

Sarah and Sevrin joined the rest of the prisoners, slumping down on the floor, backs against the wall. Sarah looked round and shivered. 'I wonder why they've brought us here?'

'I heard the soldiers say they needed workers for their rocket project. I don't mind working. They may even feed us.'

A nearby prisoner leaned across to them. He was a Kaled soldier, very young with a bleak, bitter face. Although neither of them realised it, he and Sarah had met before. The Kaled had been leader of the patrol which had emerged from the Kaled dome to capture Harry and the Doctor. Later he had been captured himself by a Thal raiding party. He gave Sevrin and

Sarah a pitying look. 'You'll work all right, muto. On the kind of job that kills you just as sure as a bullet will.'

'What work?' asked Sarah.

The young Kaled seemed to take a gloomy pleasure in breaking the bad news. 'The Thals have built a rocket. Used up the last of their manpower and resources in one final gamble. If they manage to launch it they'll wipe out the Kaled city and most of the Kaled race in one blow.'

Sarah gave him a puzzled look. 'So what are we needed for?'

'They're packing the nose-cone of the rocket with distronic explosives. To reduce weight, they're using no protective shielding. Every load we carry exposes us to distronic radiation. After two or three shifts you feel weaker. Eventually you die!'

Sarah looked at him in horror. Before she could speak a siren blared out and the prisoners shuffled wearily to their feet. She turned to the Kaled. 'What's that?'

'Rest period's over—time to start loading again.'

A Thal guard came over and prodded them to their feet with his rifle. 'All right,' snapped Sarah. 'No need to push!' She joined the long line of prisoners shuffling out of the door. Already her mind was busy with thoughts of escape.

The prisoners were marched through corridors and tunnels and finally into a huge concrete enclosure.

Sarah caught her breath. Towering far above them was the deadly silver shape of the Thal rocket. The base of the rocket was supported by a framework of scaffolding, its nose-cone touched the roof far above their heads. Sarah guessed that a section of the dome would slide back at the moment of firing. Meanwhile the rocket was securely hidden inside the Thal city dome.

Sarah noticed that the guards in here wore all-over radiation suits, gauntlets and masks. She saw too that there was a dial inset in one wall, and that the final third of it was shaded red—presumably for the danger zone.

A steel door slid back and a small lifting-truck emerged, driven by a radiation-suited guard. The truck was loaded with ingots of some dull, silvery metal, and as soon as it entered the rocket silo, the needle on the radiation dial began climbing slowly towards the danger area.

By now the prisoners had been formed into a line, with Sarah and Sevrin somewhere near the end. One by one the prisoners lifted an ingot from the truck and, hugging it to their bodies, staggered over to the doors in the base of the rocket. When it came to Sevrin's turn, he lifted the ingot with ease and set off with it. Sarah was next. She hesitated, reluctant to touch the ingot, but a guard threatened with his rifle, and she was forced to pick it up. It was astonishingly heavy for its size and she had to hug it to her body to carry it. The ingot in her arms, Sarah stumbled towards the rocket doors.

In a tiny windowless cell in the Kaled bunker, Harry Sullivan sat on a bunk and waited. It seemed ages since they had taken the Doctor away. The longer Harry waited, the more worried he became. At last he heard the thump of booted feet in the corridor outside. The cell door clanged open and the Doctor was shoved in by a guard, who promptly shut and locked the door behind him. The Doctor threw himself on the bunk with a groan of relief. Harry perched on the metal stool beside him. 'How did you get on, Doctor? Are you all right?'

The Doctor gave him a weary nod.

'Did you tell them anything?'

The Doctor managed to grin. 'I told them *everything*, every bit of scientific gobbledygook I could think of. They took *reams* of notes. Their scientific experts will be confused for *weeks*!' The Doctor chuckled. 'I learned more from them than they did from me!'

'What about this Bunker, Doctor? Where are we? What's it all for?'

'Most of the place is underground, like these cells. It's a few miles from the main Kaled dome, bomb-proof and completely impregnable to attack.'

'What are they all doing here?'

The Doctor yawned and stretched, rubbing his bruises. Harry guessed that the security guards had given him the occasional thump to loosen his tongue.

'Years ago the Kaled Government decided to form an Elite Corps. All their leading scientists, plus security men to protect them. Over the years, this Elite has become so powerful that now it can demand anything it wants . . .'

The Doctor stopped talking as they heard someone approaching outside. 'Perhaps it's the tea,' he said hopefully.

The door opened and Ronson appeared in the doorway, a guard behind him. He entered the cell and turned to the guard. 'It's all right, you needn't wait.' The man hesitated and Ronson snapped, 'I am armed. You can stay on duty outside.' The guard nodded and closed the door. Ronson looked at the Doctor stretched out on his bunk. 'I hope they didn't hurt you too much. I'm afraid I was unable to interfere.'

The Doctor waved a dismissive hand. 'I'm all right. The main thing is that you saved me from being the very first victim of a Dalek!'

Ronson started. 'How did you know that name? Just a few minutes ago, Davros announced that his new device would be known as a Dalek—an anagram of Kaled, the name of our race.'

'I have a certain advantage, in terms of time,' said the Doctor solemnly. 'In fact the reason I came was because of—well, let's say *future concern* about the development of the Daleks.'

Ronson sank wearily on to the end of the bunk. 'I too am concerned,' he confessed. 'Others feel the same, but we are powerless.'

The Doctor sat up, leaning towards him. 'Perhaps I can help. But you'll have to trust me.'

Ronson glanced towards the cell door and dropped his voice. 'We believe that Davros has changed the direction of his research into something immoral. The Elite Corps was formed to produce weapons that would win this war. But soon we saw that was futile. Already the weapons used had begun to cause genetic changes. We were forced to turn our attention to the survival of our race.'

The Doctor nodded grimly. 'Meanwhile the early products of these genetic changes—the mutos—were banished to the Wastelands?'

'That's right. Davros believed this trend was irreversible, so he decided to work *with* it, to produce accelerated mutations in an effort to find our final mutated form. He produced what he calls the ultimate creature.' Ronson rose to his feet. 'Come with me, Doctor.' He rapped on the door and the guard opened it. 'I require the assistance of these prisoners in certain top-secret experiments. You will release them into my custody.'

The guard looked doubtful, but the habit of obedience to the Scientific Elite was too strong in him. Dismissing the guard, Ronson led Harry and the Doctor in another direction. He took them along dimly-lit passages to a short corridor. The roof was supported by heavy buttresses jutting out from the walls. The corridor ended in a massive metal door in which was set a small viewing-panel, covered by a shutter.

Ronson pulled the shutter to one side, revealing a thickly-glassed window. From inside it came a pulsating green glow. 'Take a look, Doctor.'

The Doctor peered through the little window then hurriedly stepped back. Harry saw the look of revulsion on his face but couldn't resist taking a quick look through the panel. He caught a fleeting glimpse of long rows of tanks, holding twisted, hideously deformed shapes. Then the Doctor moved him aside, sliding the shutter closed. 'I shouldn't, Harry. Not unless you want to lay in a permanent stock of nightmares.'

Ronson looked at them, and Harry saw the bitterness in his face. 'You see, Doctor? If Davros has his way, that is our future. *That* is what the Kaleds will become!'

In the big communal cell, Sarah was trying to whip up a spirit of revolt. 'Look,' she said fiercely. 'We have to do something *now*. A few more shifts and we won't have the strength. We've *got* to get out of here.'

The young Kaled patrol leader glanced across at the doors. 'That's just not possible.'

Sarah looked at the guards. They were leaning against the doors, rifles held casually in the crooks of their arms. 'Oh yes, it is. Those guards aren't expecting any trouble—not from a group of worn-out slave-workers.'

'Supposing we do get out—we'll only be in the rocket silo. The exit from that goes through a Thal command point—and that'll be crawling with troops.'

'There's another way out from the silo,' replied Sarah. 'Straight up! The scaffolding goes right up to the nose-cone of the rocket. From there we could get out on to the surface of the dome, then climb down to the ground.'

Beside them the giant mutant Sevrin sat huddled beneath his all-concealing cloak and hood. 'Climb that scaffolding,' he protested mildly. 'It's very high.'

'I know,' said Sarah gently. 'I don't exactly fancy it myself. But it's our only chance to survive.' She had endured one long work-shift lugging the metal ingots into the rocket's storage chamber. The Kaled soldier had explained that while the first few shifts produced only normal fatigue, further exposure would begin a dangerous build-up of radiation effect in the body. Sarah was prepared to face any risk rather than that.

The patrol leader had already endured several shifts, and his face was grey and drawn. 'Why not,' he muttered. 'Better to take a chance than rot away here.'

'All right,' whispered Sarah. 'Now—move round among the others. Recruit as many as you can!'

Guards came in with cauldrons of grey, mushy porridge, food providing the absolute minimum of nourishment, just enough to enable the prisoners to work. Bowlfuls of the stuff were passed out and the prisoners ate greedily with their fingers, afterwards licking the bowls till they were clean. During the general confusion produced by this 'feeding time', Sevrin and the young Kaled moved among the prisoners, explaining their plan for a breakout. Some prisoners fled from them in terror, others just stared blankly. But here and there they found some willing to listen. There were still a few whose spirits were not completely broken.

When feeding was over and the bowls handed in, the three conspirators met in a corner. 'Well?' asked Sarah.

The Kaled soldier nodded fiercely. 'Some of my men were captured with me. They'll fight. So will most of the other soldiers.'

Sevrin however shook his head. 'The mutos are too frightened,' he explained sadly. 'We are always frightened. But *I* will help.'

'We'll just have to do the best we can,' Sarah said. 'Once we get started the rest will probably join in.'

The first part of the breakout was surprisingly easy. Sarah, Sevrin and the more aggressive prisoners all drifted slowly towards the door. When Sarah was opposite the nearest guard she stumbled and fell against him, pretending to faint. Instinctively the guard grabbed her—and the Kaled soldier chopped him down from behind. Before the second guard could react Sevrin sprang upon him, lifted him high in the air and dashed him to the ground. He stood looking at the motionless body as if astonished by his own daring.

'Come on,' yelled Sarah. 'Quickly!' She threw open the doors and the prisoners streamed out, overwhelming the guards on the other side. The breakout had begun!

5

Escape to Danger

The Doctor, Harry and Ronson were hurrying along the corridors beneath the Bunker. From time to time a passing guard glanced curiously at them, but the presence of one of the Scientific Elite proved a good enough passport. They talked in low voices as they walked. Ronson went on with his explanations. 'Davros says that having evolved our ultimate form, he then created a travel machine in which to house it.'

The Doctor nodded. 'And the two combined have produced a living weapon—the Daleks! He's created a monster utterly devoid of conscience. Are you prepared to help me stop him?'

'I must,' said Ronson simply. 'There are those in the Kaled government who may still have the strength to act. If they knew the full truth they could end Davros's power, close down the Bunker and disband the Elite. I myself am not allowed to leave the Bunker . . . But you two might make it.'

'Help us to escape,' urged the Doctor. 'Give me the names of the men you speak of and I promise you I'll make them listen.'

Was it going to be as easy as that, Harry wondered. He turned to Ronson. '*Can* you really get us out?'

'One of the ventilation-system ducts leads to a cave on the edge of the Wastelands. The exit is barred, but you might get through. But there's an added danger . . .'

'I knew it,' said Harry. 'Go on.'

'Some of Davros's early experiments were with our wild animals. Horrific monsters were created—some of them were allowed to live as a controlled experiment.'

'Don't tell me—they're in this cave we go through?'

Ronson nodded. Harry sighed. It certainly wasn't going to be so easy!

Ronson led them through smaller and smaller corridors, until they came to a short rock-walled tunnel. It ended in a blank wall into which was set a ventilation-duct, just large enough to admit a human body. A metal hatch covered the duct. It was stiff with disuse, and it took the Doctor and Harry quite a time to wrench it open.

As they worked, Ronson was scribbling rapidly in a plastic-covered notebook. The hatch creaked open and he handed the book to the Doctor. 'I've written down the names of all the people you should try to contact giving the facts about Davros's research, and I've added a note of introduction to confirm your story . . . If anything goes wrong . . .'

'Don't worry, I'll see it's all destroyed.' The Doctor knew that with the notebook Ronson was placing his life in their hands.

Harry jumped up to the opening and wriggled through into the cramped tunnel. Ronson helped the Doctor to climb in after him. 'Hurry,' he gasped. 'I think someone's coming. Good luck!'

The Doctor's long legs disappeared into the duct and Ronson slammed the hatch-cover closed behind them.

He turned and hurried back down the tunnel. At the point where the tunnel joined the main corridor, he ran straight into a patrolling guard. The guard was surprised to see an eminent scientist leaving what was essentially a maintenance area, but Ronson looked haughtily at him, and the man went on his way. Concealing a sigh of relief, Ronson headed back to his laboratory.

In the ventilation duct, Harry and the Doctor edged their way through total darkness. Harry didn't know which to worry about most, the perils behind them or the dangers ahead.

A yelling crowd of prisoners burst out of the cell and milled round the base of the giant rocket. Some began running blindly towards the exits, only to encounter

Thal guards running out from their command posts. The guards started shooting wildly into the crowd.

Sarah saw the young Kaled soldier fall early in the mêlée, but the giant form of Sevrin was still at her side. Together they pushed their way to the scaffolding and began climbing. Up and up they climbed, hand over hand until Sarah's arms were aching and the sounds of shooting and yelling seemed faint and distant. Gasping for breath, Sarah made the mistake of looking down. She hadn't realised how far they'd come, and the dizzying drop below her made everything spin round. Luckily Sevrin was close enough to lean across and grab her arm. 'Don't look down, Sarah. And keep climbing.'

Something bounced off the metal scaffolding near Sarah's head and whined away into space. She looked down and caught a brief glimpse of a Thal guard, his rifle pointing upwards. 'They're shooting at us,' she gasped. 'Come on.'

By now other prisoners were following their example, swarming up the scaffolding like monkeys. Many were picked off by the rifles of the Thal guards and crashed to the ground at the base of the rocket. Others were luckier, and the Thal Guard Captain soon realised there was real danger that many of his prisoners might get away. As more reinforcements arrived to deal with the prisoners, he slung his rifle over his shoulder and assembled a small group of reluctant soldiers. 'Come on—we're going up after them.' The soldiers began to climb.

High on the scaffolding, the nose-cone very close now, Sarah hung gasping. 'It's no good. I can't climb any more.'

Sevrin was close behind her. There seemed to be enormous strength in the great twisted body, and he could swing ape-like along the scaffolding with no sign of fatigue. 'You must go on, Sarah. See, they are coming after us.'

Sarah glanced down to see Thal soldiers swarming up the scaffolding in pursuit. Stronger and better fed than their escaping prisoners, they were catching up rapidly. Sarah started to climb again, but her tired sweating hands slipped on the scaffolding. She felt herself dropping into space. A sudden jerk arrested her fall. Sevrin had caught her arm, taking her whole weight with one hand while he clung to the scaffolding with his other. Sarah swung back close to the scaffolding and managed to find a fresh hold. She glanced down again. Because of the delay, the pursuing Thals were now much closer. Yet the narrow escape had stiffened Sarah's determination not to be recaptured; she began climbing even higher. There wasn't far to go.

At the top of the scaffolding, Sevrin was waiting for her. They were right by the nose-cone of the rocket, and the roof of the dome was only a few feet away. 'Look, Sarah. There's a section of the dome that slides away. We could reach it from the tip of the nose-cone and get out!'

63

'How do we get on to the nose-cone?'

'We'll have to jump for it—I'll go first, then I can catch you.'

Sevrin poised himself for a moment, then leaped like a giant spider across the gap between the scaffolding and the nose-cone. He landed spread-eagled on the very tip of the rocket, hands scrabbling for a hold on the smoothly polished metal. When he felt secure he yelled. 'It's all right, Sarah. Jump and I'll catch you.'

Sarah looked across. The gap seemed enormous, and stretching down below her was the entire length of the huge rocket. The figures round its base seemed like tiny moving dots. She clung to the scaffolding, shivering with fear.

'You've got to do it,' called Sevrin. 'Jump!'

Sarah looked down again. The pursuing Thal soldiers were very close. She jumped. She hit the nose-cone with a thump, and immediately started sliding off, but one of Sevrin's huge hands caught her and dragged her to safety on its rounded tip. A narrow ledge gave a foothold. 'We're nearly there,' he muttered reassuringly. 'Just a bit more and we'll be on the dome surface. We'll be safe.' Slowly Sevrin climbed to his feet. Balancing precariously on the very tip of the rocket's nose-cone he slid back the panel in the dome. Sarah felt a rush of cold air and saw the night sky through the gap. Sevrin had one hand on the edge of the gap, and was reaching down to pull Sarah through when a voice called out, 'That's far enough.'

The Thal soldiers had caught up with them. The Guard Captain was clinging to the scaffolding with one hand, levelling his rifle at them with the other. Close to him, the rest of his men were doing the same. 'Right,' he ordered. 'Back on the scaffolding.'

Sevrin sighed. Releasing his grip on the opening he took a flying leap and landed back on the scaffolding. Immediately a Thal soldier jammed a rifle in his ribs. 'Start climbing. No tricks, or you'll go down the quick way.' Obediently Sevrin started to descend.

The Guard Captain turned to Sarah. 'Now you.'

Hanging grimly on to the nose-cone, Sarah didn't dare move. 'All right,' said the Captain softly, 'I'll come and get you.' He leaped confidently across the gap and landed on the rounded tip of the rocket where Sevrin had stood a moment earlier. 'Take my hand,' he ordered. Sarah reached up and he grasped her wrist. Suddenly he jerked. Sarah's feet slid from her precarious foothold. She was dangling over empty space supported by the Captain's hand.

The Guard Captain knew he would be punished because of the prisoners' revolt, and the knowledge made him cruel. He grinned down at Sarah. 'All I have to do is slacken my grip . . . They say people who fall from great heights are dead before they hit the ground. I don't believe that, do you?' He pretended to let Sarah go and she moaned in fear. Tiring of his game the Captain pulled her back to safety. 'Don't worry, you're going back to work. Before long you'll wish I *had* let you drop.' He called across to one of the soldiers. 'Better throw a rope over, or this one will never make it down.' As the rope was lashed round her Sarah felt only relief. The escape had failed—but she was still alive.

Harry felt the journey through the cramped dark tunnel was never going to end. Maybe they were lost, he thought, maybe they'd die here in these tunnels. Suddenly he felt cold, damp air, and saw a dim glow of light. 'I think we're nearly there, Doctor,' he called behind him. The tunnel widened a little towards its end, which was blocked by heavy wire mesh.

The Doctor squeezed up beside Harry. 'That must be the entrance to the cave. So all we've got to do is . . .' A snuffling grunt came out of the darkness.

'Must be one of Davros's little pets,' Harry whispered nervously. They waited in silence. Something big and shapeless brushed past the other side of the grille, and they heard it shamble away into the darkness. They waited a moment longer.

'Well, whatever it was, it's gone,' the Doctor said cheerfully. 'Give me a hand, Harry.' Using their combined strength, they managed to prise off the grille.

'After you, Doctor,' said Harry politely.

The Doctor grinned and slipped into the cave. Harry followed him. The cave was very dark, and he was aware of little more than a dank rock wall close beside him. But there did seem to be a lighter patch somewhere in the distance. The Doctor tapped his shoulder. 'Keep close to the wall, Harry, and make for the light.'

As they shuffled along, Harry was almost grateful for the darkness. Whatever was in the cave, he thought he'd be a lot happier if he *didn't* see it. They reached the light source without incident. It proved to be a very small barred window looking out on to the Wastelands.

'We've made it,' said Harry exultantly. 'Come on, Doctor.' He hurried towards the window. The Doctor was peering cautiously at the ground just beneath the window. A giant round shape was half-buried in the ground.

'Harry, be careful——' the Doctor called. But he was too late. The hump seemed to split into two separate halves. They widened like gaping jaws and clashed down on Harry's leg. Harry let out a howl of pain and the Doctor ran to his side.

Harry's leg was gripped tight by what appeared to be a kind of giant clam, several feet across. Hissing fiercely the creature was trying to drag Harry into the darkness of the cave, no doubt hoping to digest him at leisure. The Doctor grabbed a chunk of rock and hammered at the shell, but it was iron-hard. Remorselessly the sliding horror dragged Harry further away. The Doctor glanced round for a weapon. He saw a jagged spear-like piece of rock projecting from one wall. Using his rock as a hammer he broke it away, ran back to Harry and jammed the improvised spear into the gap in the giant shell. He rammed the sharp stone deep inside the clam, using all his strength. With a hiss of pain, the 'jaws' sprang open. Harry fell backwards, free, and the creature slithered away in the darkness.

The Doctor knelt beside Harry who was moaning and clutching his leg. He made a brief examination. 'Nasty bruise there, but nothing seems to be broken,' he said briskly. 'You had a lucky escape, Harry. That must have been one of Davros's nastier experiments.'

Harry rubbed his leg tenderly. 'Why is it always me who puts his foot in it?' he grumbled.

The Doctor slapped him on the back. 'You'll be all right, Harry. Can you walk yet?'

'Just about.' Harry hobbled a few steps.

'Then we'd better get out of here. It's not a place to hang about.'

As they wrenched at the rusting bars in the window Harry said, 'When we're out in the Wastelands, Doctor, can't we have a look for Sarah?'

The Doctor shook his head. 'At the moment we're just a couple of fugitives. We'd be shot or imprisoned in no time. There's still a war going on, remember. But if we warn the Kaled Government about Davros—well, they'll owe us a favour, won't they? We can ask for an official search.'

Harry looked worried and the Doctor gave him a reassuring grin.

'Don't worry, Harry, we'll find her, I promise you. But one problem at a time. And our problem now is to get past these bars.'

In the Bunker's main laboratory, Davros was holding a demonstration. This time *two* Daleks were gliding backwards and forwards along the laboratory. They completed a complicated sequence of evolutions, then came to a halt before Davros's chair. The granting voice of the nearer one said, 'We await your commands.'

Chillingly like that of his creation, the voice of Davros spoke, 'No further command. Disengage automotive circuits.' The lights on the Daleks' heads went out, their guns and sucker-arms drooped. 'Excellent,' said Davros in a satisfied voice.

One of his retinue of scientists, a plump, smooth little man called Kavell, leaned forward obsequiously. 'They are perfect, Davros. A truly brilliant creation.'

The rasping voice corrected him. 'A brilliant creation, yes. But not perfect. Scientist-Technicians!' Davros raised his hand and a group of younger men hurried forward. 'Improvements must be made in the optical systems and the sensory circuits. Their instincts must be as accurate as any scientific instrument. Work will begin at once. You will carry out the following adjustments . . .'

As Davros's voice droned on, Kavell slipped away from the group and moved across to the corner desk where Ronson sat working. He peered over Ronson's shoulders as if checking his results, and said quietly, 'Does Davros know that your two alien prisoners have escaped?'

Ronson glanced up quickly, then went on with his work. 'As far as I know the prisoners are in their cell.'

'Don't worry, Ronson, I won't betray you. You're not the only one worried about Davros's plans. Now answer me. Does Davros know?'

'The prisoners are in their cell,' repeated Ronson. He didn't trust Kavell enough to make any damaging admissions.

The plump little man chuckled. 'I have some news for you, Ronson. Your two prisoners have managed to cross the Wastelands and make contact with certain members of the Government.'

'How do you know that?'

Kavell smiled complacently. 'There are still some advantages to being in charge of the communications system.' He looked across the laboratory to where Davros sat surrounded by his admiring assistants. 'All we can do now is hope that your friends manage to convince our leaders that Davros's work must be ended.'

Kavell walked away, and Ronson buried his head in his hands. 'They must succeed,' he muttered to himself. 'They *must*!'

In the Kaled City, Harry Sullivan sat in a luxurious underground conference room, scarcely able to believe what was happening. Only the Doctor could possibly have managed it, thought Harry. No one else would have the cheek!

When the window bars had finally given way, the Doctor had led Harry across the Wastelands to one of the main entrances to the Kaled City. Marching straight up to an astonished sentry, the Doctor had demanded to see his superior officer. Then he had bullied his way up the chain of command, intimidating a Captain, a Colonel and finally a full-blown General, with impressive but vague talk of a vitally important top-secret mission, and repeated demands to be put in touch with certain important members of the Kaled Government, dropping their names freely, as if they were old friends.

Several times Harry felt that various officers had been on the point of having them shot, but the Doctor's bare-faced audacity had at last succeeded. They had been granted an interview with Mogran, one of the names on Ronson's list.

Mogran had listened sceptically at first, then with increasing concern. He had studied the letter and the details of Davros's experiments in Ronson's notebook. Finally he had summoned a secret meeting in this hidden conference room.

Now Mogran was addressing his fellow councillors, while the Doctor waited beside him. Harry was amused to see that Ravon, the young General from whom they'd first escaped, was also at the meeting, puzzled to find his former prisoners being treated as honoured guests.

Mogran, an impressively robed figure with silver hair, was concluding his speech, '. . . and it is only because I am personally convinced of both the accuracy and importance of the Doctor's information that I ask you to listen to him now. Doctor?'

The Doctor stepped forward, as relaxed and authoritative as the guest-of-honour on some state occasion. 'Some of what I am about to tell you concerns events in the future. Events not only on this planet, but on other planets whose existence is not even known to you . . .'

A murmur of surprise went up from the audience. The Doctor raised his hand. 'I realise that may be hard to accept, but my knowledge is based firmly on scientific fact. I *know* that Davros is creating a machine creature, a monster that will terrorise and destroy millions. He has given this vile creature a name—a name that is a distortion of that of your own race—DALEK! The word is new to you, but for a thousand generations it will bring fear and terror.' The Doctor paused impressively. 'Davros has one of the finest scientific minds in existence. But he has a fanatical desire to perpetuate himself in his creation. He is without conscience, without soul and without pity, and his creations are equally devoid of these qualities . . .'

As the Doctor went on with his speech, Harry slumped down in his seat. Would the Doctor be able to convince them? The fate of this world, and of many more, depended on his success . . .

6

Betrayal

Davros watched with satisfaction as a team of scientists and technicians toiled to make the improvements he had demanded for his Daleks. Through the vision-lens that provided him with sight, he saw Security-Commander Nyder enter the laboratory and come towards him. Davros wheeled his chair to a secluded corner, and Nyder joined him. He leaned forward urgently, keeping his voice low. 'Davros, I've just had word from one of our supporters in the Government. Your old enemy Councillor Mogran has called a meeting. Only known opponents of your Scientific Elite have been invited to attend.'

Davros clenched and unclenched his withered hand. 'I want a full report of everything that's discussed. I don't care how you get the information . . . just get it!' After a moment he went on more calmly. 'I don't think we need be too concerned. Many times in the past fifty years opponents in the Government have tried to interfere with my research. They have always failed – they will fail again.'

'There's something else,' Nyder said. 'The two alien prisoners left in Ronson's charge. They are attending the meeting.'

Davros turned his chair so that he could see Ronson working in the corner. Nyder followed the direction of his gaze. 'What action shall I take concerning the traitor Ronson?' The lipless mouth of Davros twitched in what might have been a smile.

'For the moment, none. I shall deal with him in my own way.'

The meeting was drawing to its close. The Kaled politicians were talking among themselves, occasionally glancing across to the Doctor and Harry. General Ravon, who seemed to take no part in the deliberations, was standing nearby. Harry wondered if he was guarding them. The suspense was getting on his nerves. 'Do you think you convinced them, Doctor?' he whispered.

'I'm not sure, Harry, I tried, but sometimes words just aren't enough.'

Harry saw a bustle of movement on the other side of the conference room. 'Looks as if they've reached a decision.'

With muttered farewells the other councillors were hurrying away, leaving Mogran behind. He came over to the Doctor, who jumped eagerly to his feet. 'Well, what have you decided?'

'It has been agreed that an independent tribunal will investigate the work being carried out at the Bunker.'

'That could take months,' protested the Doctor. 'Davros has prototype Daleks ready for action *now*!'

Mogran held up his hand. 'It has also been agreed that pending the result of the investigation, Davros's Dalek experiments will be suspended.'

The Doctor brightened. 'Now that's more like it—though mind you, it's less than I'd hoped for . . .'

Mogran gave him the reassuring smile of a politician. 'I assure you, Doctor, if your allegations are borne out the Bunker will be closed down, and Davros dismissed. Meanwhile, you are welcome to remain here as our guests.'

'I'm afraid we haven't time for that,' the Doctor said briskly. 'One of my companions was lost in the Wastelands almost as soon as we arrived. I'd be very glad if you'd give us some help in finding her.'

Mogran looked ill-at-ease. Glancing round for a solution he caught sight of General Ravon, and passed the buck with polished skill. 'I'm afraid that's outside my sphere. But General Ravon here will give you all the help he can. I must go and inform Davros of my Committee's decision.' Mogran left the room, and Harry turned aggressively to Ravon. He didn't much fancy leaving Sarah's fate in the hands of one who'd so recently been their enemy.

'Well, General,' he demanded, '*can* you help us?'

'As a matter of fact, I believe I can,' Ravon replied surprisingly. 'One of our agents inside the Thal dome sent a report about a newly arrived girl prisoner who led some kind of breakout among the slave-workers. Gave the Thals a lot of trouble before she was recaptured.'

Harry said eagerly, 'Well, that certainly *sounds* like Sarah. What's all this about slaves?'

'The Thals are using prisoners to load their last great rocket. It's their super-weapon. They think they'll win the war with it.'

'You don't seem very worried.'

Ravon smiled confidently. 'No matter how powerful the rocket, it will never penetrate our protective dome. Davros had it reinforced with a protective coating, a new substance with the strength of thirty-foot concrete.'

'Congratulations,' said the Doctor drily. 'Now how can you help us find Sarah?'

Ravon looked doubtful. 'One of my agents could get you into the service shafts under the Thal rocket silo. But after that, you'd be on your own.'

'Understood,' said the Doctor. 'Let's be on our way.'

He seemed ready to set off at once. Harry caught his arm. 'I'm as anxious to rescue Sarah as you are, Doctor, but do you think there'd be time for a bite to eat first? It's been all go since we arrived.'

The Doctor looked at Ravon who said, 'Yes, of course. Come with me and I'll arrange it.'

As they followed him from the room Harry said, 'I suppose we'll have to cross those Wastelands again.'

'That's right.' The Doctor smiled. 'And then our troubles will really begin.' You might almost have thought he was looking forward to it.

Councillor Mogran was an extremely worried man. Somehow everything was going far too smoothly. He'd expected fiercely determined opposition from Davros. Instead he was encountering an unnerving degree of co-operation. 'An investigation?' Davros was saying. 'But of course, Councillor Mogran. I welcome your inquiry into my work here. The Kaled people sacrifice much to give us the materials we need. They have a right to know how our work is proceeding. My only hope is that when they learn of our achievements their patriotism will be re-fired.'

Mogran could say little in face of such sentiments. 'I am grateful for the way you have accepted this decision, Davros. There is one thing more—until the inquiry is concluded, all work on the Daleks must be suspended.'

'If that is your wish, then I must obey. It will take time to close down certain equipment. Shall we say twenty-four hours?'

The request was so reasonable that Mogran did not dare to refuse it entirely. 'Shall we say *twelve* hours?' he countered.

'It will be difficult—but it will be done.'

Mogran prepared to leave. 'Then it remains only for me to thank you for your co-operation.'

Davros bowed his ghastly skull-like head. 'It is simply my duty. The investigation will reveal only my loyalty and total dedication to our cause.'

Mogran left the laboratory. Nyder, who had been a silent witness to the confrontation, leaned over Davros's chair. 'We cannot allow this investigation. The stupidest councillors cannot fail to see that the Daleks will give *you* total power. They will end the experiment.'

'There will *be* no investigation,' Davros answered. 'Mogran has just signed the death-warrant of his city. Only we, the Elite, will go on.'

Nyder looked at him in astonishment, but said nothing.

'I want twenty of the genetically-mutated creatures installed in the machines immediately. They will be our shock-troops in the battle for survival.'

'They're still erratic, mentally unstable,' Nyder protested.

'They will not be allowed *total* self-control. I shall prepare a computer programme to limit their actions. Come, Nyder. We are going on a journey!'

The Doctor and Harry were close to their destination— the Thal rocket silo where they hoped to find and rescue Sarah. After a hasty meal, Ravon had handed them over to one of his agents, a weasel-faced man who spoke only when strictly necessary. Disguised in the hooded cloaks of mutos, the Doctor and Harry had been led by way of hidden paths and abandoned trenches across the central Wastelands to the outskirts of the Thal dome. Shifting a carefully-hidden hatchway, the agent had then gone underground, leading them through an interminable series of cramped tunnels and passageways where mysterious machinery hummed and throbbed. Finally he had stopped in a corridor junction, pointing to a ladder, bolted to the wall, which gave access to a hatch-cover. 'You're right underneath the silo now. That's all I can do for you. Here's your map!' And with that he had slipped away into the darkness.

Harry and the Doctor stripped off their muto disguise. 'Well, might as well get on with it,' said the Doctor. He climbed the ladder till he was high enough to raise the hatch-cover a few inches and peep through the gap. 'Seems clear enough. Come on, Harry.' Carefully the Doctor lifted the hatch and climbed through, reaching down to help Harry after him. They replaced the cover and looked at their surroundings.

They were in a featureless concrete corridor. Nearby was a door, the top-half glassed in. A notice read, 'Launch Control'. The Doctor checked his map. 'We seem to have surfaced in the administrative block,' he whispered. 'But we're pretty near the rocket.'

Impelled by his usual curiosity, the Doctor couldn't resist a swift peep through the glass panel in the Launch Control door. He stiffened in sudden surprise and beckoned Harry over. Harry joined him. The place was crowded with all the paraphernalia of a rocket control room, but now it was full of people too. Some wore military uniform, others robes like those of Kaled councilmen, though of different design. They were surrounding two central figures, who were set apart from the rest. To Harry's astonishment he saw Davros, in his wheelchair, Nyder beside him. He nudged the Doctor. 'What's the chief scientist of the Kaleds doing in the Thal rocket base?'

The Doctor touched a finger to his lips. With infinite caution he opened the door the merest crack, and Harry heard the metallic, inhuman tones of Davros. '. . . my concern is only for peace, for an end to the carnage that has virtually destroyed *both* races.'

Davros was talking to a high-ranking Thal Minister, summoned specially for this incredible meeting. Like his Kaled opposite number, Mogran, the Minister was a tall, imposing man with an air of great authority. There was scepticism in his voice. 'Why not try to convince the Kaled government to make peace?'

'I have tried, time and time again. They will settle for nothing less than total extermination of the Thals.'

Davros's deliberately provocative announcement was greeted with angry murmurings. 'Then they deserve to perish,' the Minister replied coldly. 'And perish they shall. Our rocket——'

'—will be a total failure.' The voice of Davros completed the sentence. 'The Kaled city dome cannot be penetrated. It is protected by a special material of my invention. Your rocket will hardly scratch it—unless you accept my help.' Nyder produced a sheaf of papers and held them out. 'This is the measure of our sincerity. A simple chemical formula. Load the substance into normal artillery shells and bombard the Kaled dome. The dome will be weakened, its molecular structure made brittle. Then your rocket will penetrate with virtually no resistance.'

The Minister took the papers and looked at them incredulously. 'Why do you give us this information, when it means the end of your city?'

'No price is too great for peace,' Davros said solemnly. 'When the war is finally over, I ask only to be allowed to take part in the reconstruction of our world. And, remember, by dawn tomorrow this planet could be at peace.'

The Minister spoke slowly, 'If you would give me a moment to confer with my colleagues alone?'

Davros's chair began moving towards the door. The Doctor and Harry ducked back, and disappeared round the corner. After a moment they heard Nyder's lowered voice. 'Do you think they believed you, Davros?'

'They are hungry for victory. They will use the formula, and fire their rocket, no matter what they think.'

The door opened and again they heard the Minister's voice. 'A barrage of shells containing the formula will begin at once. The rocket launch will follow immediately. I shall see that you are given safe escort from the city.'

As the Minister led his two visitors away, the Doctor and Harry emerged from hiding. 'We'll have to warn the Kaleds,' muttered the Doctor.

'Not before we find Sarah,' Harry said firmly.

'Of course not,' agreed the Doctor. 'Come on, Harry, don't just stand there.'

Guided by the Kaled spy's map, they made their way along the corridors towards the rocket. Suddenly the Doctor heard footsteps approaching from an intersecting corridor. He peered round the corner and saw two Thal guards, both dressed in anti-radiation suits, marching along the corridor towards him. He ducked back, whispered a few words to Harry, and then stepped blithely round the corner. Hat on the back of his head, long scarf dangling, the Doctor had passed the two guards before they had time to take in his extraordinary appearance. As soon as it did register, both guards spun round, rifles levelled. 'Hey,' called one of them. 'Who are you?'

The Doctor walked back towards them, his eyes wide and innocent. 'Well, as a matter of fact I'm a spy.

I wonder if you could help me—I'm looking for this rocket of yours . . .'

The astonished guard gaped at him—giving Harry Sullivan time to fell him with a rabbit-punch below the ear. The first guard dropped, the second turned—and the Doctor knocked him out. They dragged their victims round the corner and out of sight.

Beneath the towering bulk of the huge rocket, the motley band of slave workers were coming to the end of their task. Sarah staggered wearily as she came out of the rocket. Sevrin caught her by the arm, supporting her. One of the guards laughed. 'Don't worry, that was the last consignment. You can have all the rest you need now.'

As the prisoners came out of the rocket they were bunched into a group under the rifles of a couple of guards. The rest of the Thal soldiers marched away. Sarah looked at Sevrin. 'If the rocket is loaded, why are they keeping us here?'

The giant muto shrugged. 'Why should they bother to move us?'

Sarah looked up at the rocket. 'But when that thing goes off, we'll all be killed.'

'Our lives are of no more interest to them.'

Sevrin seemed resigned to his fate, but Sarah certainly was not. Their second shift on the rocket had been a fairly short one, and so far Sarah was feeling no ill effects other than normal tiredness. She was fairly sure her exposure had been too short to do serious damage, and she was by no means ready to abandon hope of escape.

She looked round. Only two guards now—they could always have another go at breaking out. Her heart sank as two more guards in radiation suits walked into the silo. They walked up to the soldiers guarding the prisoners, then suddenly jumped them. There was a flurry of blows and the Thal soldiers were knocked out. The new arrivals started removing their radiation suits. To her amazement and delight, Sarah found herself looking at the Doctor and Harry Sullivan.

The Doctor ran across and gave her a hug. 'Are you all right, Sarah?'

'I am now,' she said. 'But we've got to get out of here. The Thals are just about to set this rocket off.'

'I know. Sarah, you've got to go with Harry. Harry, here's the map, you can find a way out. Get to the Kaled dome and tell General Ravon what we've learned. He must evacuate at once.'

Sarah looked at the Doctor sadly, realising that their reunion was to be very brief. 'What are you going to do?'

'I'll try to sabotage the rocket and delay the launch. There's no time to argue, off you go!' He turned to the other prisoners. 'Go on, all of you—you're free. Escape while you can.'

Dazedly the prisoners began stumbling off. Sarah noticed a bewildered Sevrin staring about. 'You come with us, Sevrin,' she called. The muto moved over to join them.

The Doctor waved his arms. 'Off you go, the lot of you—I've work to do.'

Sarah still hesitated, but he was obviously quite determined. Harry took her arm. 'Come along, old girl, or we'll all be caught.' Sarah allowed him to lead her away.

Harry took Sarah and Sevrin out of the silo and along the corridors. His eyes were on the ground and he stopped when he saw a hatch like the one they'd emerged from. 'This'll do.' With Sevrin helping, Harry lifted the hatch and sent first Sevrin, then Sarah down into the darkness of the service tunnel. Just as he was about to climb down himself, Thal soldiers ran round the corner, firing as they came. Harry bolted through the hatchway, bullets whizzing over his head, landing on top of Sarah and Sevrin. 'Come on, they're after us,' he yelled. The three disentangled themselves and set off along the tunnel at a run.

In the silo the Doctor heard the sound of firing and hoped his friends were still safe. Then he dismissed them from his mind, reserving all his concentration for the task at hand. He studied the rocket thoughtfully. Perhaps if he started by severing the exterior fuel lines . . . The Doctor took a knife from the body of an unconscious guard and purposefully approached the massive tail fin of the rocket. He leaned forward, jabbed with the knife . . . there was a sudden shower of blue sparks, and a crackling noise. Twisting in agony, the Doctor's body was thrown clear across the silo. He crashed to the ground and lay still.

In the Rocket control room, a technician studied a flickering dial. 'Better check the silo,' he called to a guard. 'Someone's trying sabotage.'

The Thal Minister, waiting to watch the launch, said anxiously, 'Any damage?'

The technician shook his head. 'He ran into our electrical defence system. Probably dead by now.'

In the silo, guards were running towards the motionless body of the Doctor.

7

Countdown to Destruction

The Doctor heard a voice moaning and muttering. 'Must stop rocket . . . warn . . .' To his surprise he realised the voice was his own.

There came another voice. 'Still alive is he? A shock like that should have killed him immediately.'

Then a gruffer voice, 'What do we do with him, Minister?'

'Oh, I've no time now,' said the first voice fussily. 'Leave him where he is till after the launch. I'll interrogate him myself if I've time. Otherwise you chaps can have him.'

The Doctor opened his eyes cautiously, then closed them again, since the whole room was spinning like a Catherine wheel. He made a mighty effort and tried again, first one eye then the other. He was in the rocket control room, the room in which he'd watched Davros betray his people not so long ago. But he couldn't move . . .

The Doctor realised that he had been lashed by the arms into a wheeled metal chair and shoved into a corner, a piece of unimportant, unfinished business to be dealt with later. The room was a bustle of activity as civilian and military VIPs got in the way of the technical staff desperately preparing for the countdown.

The Minister was looking at a monitor screen which showed a picture of the Kaled City beneath its protective dome. The dome was in a bad state now, broken in several places, with a creeping stain spreading over its surface. 'It's working,' said the minister exultantly. 'The Kaled dome is breaking up. Start the countdown!'

Helpless in his chair the Doctor shouted, 'No— you mustn't.' No one took any notice—except for the guard, who gave him an absent-minded cuff to silence him. Everyone was intent on the big digital clock which dominated the main control panel. It was counting down from fifty—forty-nine, forty-eight, forty-seven . . .

Other monitors were alive now, showing the missile on its launch-pad. The clock was still counting down, through the thirties, twenties, into single figures . . . ten, nine, eight, seven, six, five . . .

Using the wall behind him as a lever, the Doctor kicked fiercely backwards, sending his wheeled chair skidding into the main control console. He lashed frantically with his feet at the instrument panel, but the guard pulled him back, and the Doctor's feet flailed uselessly in the air. Two . . . one . . . blast-off! Helplessly the Doctor watched as the missile lifted from its pad and set off on the brief journey towards the Kaled dome.

Now everyone's attention shifted back to the monitors showing the dome as, battered and broken, it awaited final destruction. There was a blinding flash, a distant explosion that shook the control room. When the smoke cleared the Kaled dome had disappeared.

Flames roared in the crater that had replaced it, like those of some newly-born volcano.

Cheers and shouts echoed through the Thal control room. Only the Doctor sat silent, his head slumped on his chest, appalled as always by the corrupting brutality of war. Thousands of their fellow-creatures dead, and these people were cheering. On top of that, there was his own, personal loss. He had sent Sarah and Harry back to the Kaled city – the city that was now no more than a guttering inferno on the monitor screen.

The same terrible picture was seen on another monitor screen, this one in Davros's Bunker, some miles from the Kaled city. The Bunker had been far enough away, and sufficiently deep underground to escape the effects of the rocket. Davros and his Elite Corps of scientists and security men were quite unharmed.

Davros wheeled his chair away from the screen. 'Switch it off,' he ordered, and one of the scientists hurried to obey. Davros turned to the awe-stricken group around him. 'Never fear, my friends. We shall avenge the destruction of our city with retaliation so massive and so merciless that it will live in history.' He touched the control on his chair-arm and a group of three Daleks glided into the laboratory. They formed a line before Davros, awaiting his commands. Davros looked round the room. 'Let our vengeance begin with the destruction of the Thal agent, Ronson. It was he who betrayed us to the Thals. He gave them the formula which made possible the destruction of our beloved city.'

Gliding smoothly, the line of Daleks swung round to encircle Ronson, who cowered back into his corner. 'No, no,' he babbled. 'It isn't true . . .'

Viciously Davros hissed, 'Exterminate! Exterminate! Exterminate!'

The Dalek guns blazed and Ronson was hurled across the room. His body collapsed, a charred and smoking ruin, against the far wall. Davros spoke, not to the horrified Thal scientists, but to the Daleks. 'Today the Kaled city and much of the Kaled race has ended, consumed in the fires of war. But from the ashes will rise the supreme creature, the ultimate conqueror of the Universe—the Dalek!'

No one moved or spoke. Still ignoring the scientists, Davros addressed his creations. 'Today you begin a journey that will take the Daleks to their destiny of universal and absolute supremacy. You have been programmed to complete a task. You will now begin.'

In response to Davros's speech the leading Dalek spoke only two words. But in them was the whole of the Dalek creed. In that grinding, metallic voice, so hideously like Davros's own, it said, 'We obey.' The Daleks turned and glided from the laboratory.

In the Thal rocket control room, the rejoicing went on. Wine was produced, toasts were drunk. No one thought about the Doctor, slumped head-down in his corner.

The Minister was in the full flood of his eloquence. 'A thousand years of war, and now it's ended. Listen to the people, they know already.' From outside the control room came a growing rumble of distant cheering, as the good news spread through the Thal City. 'I must speak to them,' said the Minister. 'There must be a victory parade. Come, there is much to be done . . .'

He began to lead his fellow VIPs from the room. As they passed the Doctor, one of the Minister's special aides, a tall, severe-looking girl called Bettan, asked, 'What about him?'

The Minister glared indignantly at the Doctor. 'He must be punished, executed . . .' The Minister broke off. He was a kindly man at heart, and he really wasn't in the mood to think about such distasteful matters as executions. 'No—let us show that although ruthless in war, we Thals can be merciful in victory. All political prisoners will be freed, and all charges dropped. Release him!' The Minister swept out, and at a nod from Bettan the guard began untying the Doctor. He rose and stretched his tall figure, his face sad. Bettan turned to go, then hesitated. There was something curiously compelling about this odd-looking man in the strange clothes.

'You had friends in the Kaled City?' she said gently.

'Two people very dear to me. The worst of it is, I sent them back into—that.' He glanced at the monitor where the ruined remains of the Kaled city could be seen, still burning fiercely.

'What will you do now?'

'Start again. Try to complete what I came here to do.'

'What was that?' Bettan asked curiously.

'Stop the development of the Daleks, the machine creatures Davros has created. Creatures as evil as he is himself.'

'Davros is interested only in achieving peace. *He* told us how to destroy the Kaled dome,' Bettan protested.

The Doctor shook his head emphatically. 'The Kaleds themselves realised the danger of Davros's experiments. They were about to stop him. Rather than let that happen, he betrayed his own people.'

'You'll never convince the Thals that Davros is evil,' said Bettan. 'He's become a popular hero!'

The Doctor nodded, lost in thought.

'You're *free* now,' said Bettan. 'You can go where you please.'

'Thank you,' the Doctor said absently. With a sudden, charming smile, he wandered away.

Bettan was an efficient and hard-working young woman, with an important official position. Arrangements for the victory celebrations kept her busy during the next few hours. But she often found herself thinking of the strange man in the control room. She had no idea of the terrifying circumstances under which she was to meet him again.

'And there you have it, gentlemen. That outlines the chromosomal variations to be introduced into the genetic structuring of the embryo Daleks. They are to be implemented at once.' Through his vision-lens, Davros looked irritably around the small group of leading scientists. Their faces did not hold the approval and adulation to which he had become accustomed. Instead they looked shocked, disapproving even. It was Gharman, the group leader, who spoke for the rest.

'Davros . . . the changes you outline will create enormous mental defects.'

'They will not be defects—they will be improvements,' snapped the metallic voice.

'It will mean creatures without conscience. No sense of right or wrong, no pity. They'll be completely without feeling or emotion.'

'That is correct. That is the purpose of the changes. See that they are carried out—without question, Gharman.'

No one dared object further, and the scientists left to begin their tasks. Nyder, who had entered in time to witness the end of this scene, smiled thinly and went over to Davros. 'The Dalek task-force is in position,' he said. 'They await your order.'

'I see no reason for further delay.' The withered hand dropped down on a control. Miles away, on the edge of the Thal city, Daleks began to move forward.

The Doctor made his way with difficulty through the rejoicing Thal city. The place was completely roofed-in, like one enormous building. Corridors, streets, squares and walk-ways were jammed with excited revellers, all celebrating the end of a war which had been going on their whole lives. It was rather like being forced to attend an enormous noisy party when not really in the mood. People hugged the Doctor, slapped him on the back and even tried to kiss him. Others pressed food and drink on him, and urged him to join parties in their homes.

Slowly the Doctor forged ahead, accepting some refreshment, but smilingly refusing all other invitations. At last, as he came to the edge of the city, things were a little quieter. The Doctor was looking for a way out into the Wastelands. He intended to make his way to Davros's bunker, though he had no very clear idea what he would do when he got there.

Dodging a group of revellers dancing in a city square, the Doctor moved on. He could still hear the sound of shouts and laughter behind him. Suddenly, silence fell. Then there were screams, shouts of terror. The Doctor ran back the way he had come. Turning into the little square he stopped appalled. The bodies of the dancers were strewn all over the square, contorted in attitudes of sudden death. A Dalek was methodically shooting down the fleeing survivors. A second Dalek glided out to join it. Across the square came the familiar hated voices. 'Exterminate! Exterminate! Exterminate!'

The Doctor turned and ran back towards the gate. There was nothing he could possibly do here. It was all the more urgent that he tackle the evil at its source.

As the Doctor ran he heard shouts and screams of terror from all over the city. He could easily guess what was happening. The happy, careless Thals, the sinister shapes gliding from the shadows, the cries of 'Exterminate!' and the blazing Dalek guns . . . Then the heaps of charred, smoking bodies as the Daleks moved off to continue their dreadful work . . .

The main gate of the Thal city stood open and unguarded. No wonder the Daleks had entered so easily. As the Doctor ran up to the gate he collided with a fleeing figure. It was Bettan, the girl he had seen in the control room. She clutched his arm. 'There are— *machines* all over the city. Killing everybody without

97

mercy. Are those the things you told me about, the things you said Davros made?'

The Doctor grabbed her and pulled her into the shelter of a doorway. A line of sinister metal shapes glided into the square, driving before them a group of running figures. Dalek guns opened fire, the fleeing Thals twisted and fell. The Doctor and Bettan froze motionless in their doorway. The Daleks surveyed the square a moment longer, then turned and glided back into the city. Only then did the Doctor answer Bettan's question. 'Yes,' he said softly. 'Those are the Daleks. Come on, we'll be safer in the Wastelands than here.' They made their way out through the gates and across the Wastelands.

Soon the city was invisible behind them, lost in the perpetual fog and darkness of the Wastelands. They found an abandoned trench and sat down to rest. Bettan was still unable to take in what had happened. 'Davros didn't need to go that far. When our leaders saw they were beaten they would have surrendered.'

'Perhaps they tried,' said the Doctor. 'The Daleks accept no terms. Davros has conditioned them to wipe the Thals from this planet.'

'Some of us will survive,' Bettan said fiercely. 'And we'll fight back.'

The Doctor looked hard at her. 'Do you mean that? Are you really prepared to help me?'

'I'll do anything I can.'

'Even go back to the city?'

Bettan winced, but her voice was steady. 'Even that . . . if it'll really help.'

The Doctor leaned forward. 'To destroy the Daleks, we must destroy Davros himself,' he said urgently. 'I'm going to go back into the Bunker and do whatever I can. But I need the backing of some kind of fighting force.' Bettan looked puzzled.

'What can I do?'

'You said yourself, there are bound to be *some* survivors. If you could organise them, find arms and explosives, make an attack on Davros's Bunker—it could be the diversion I'll need. As yet there aren't so many Daleks in existence. If you stay out of their way there's a chance. Will you try it?' Bettan nodded. She stood up. 'Goodbye—and good luck.'

Bettan slipped out of the trench and began retracing their steps, back towards the city. As she came within sight of the main gate she saw Daleks gliding through the streets, illuminated by the flames of the burning buildings. Dodging from one hiding place to another, she made her way back to the city centre, steeling herself against the horrors she would find inside.

The Doctor meanwhile moved across the Wastelands in the opposite direction. He was working his way along a slit-trench that seemed to run in the right direction, when suddenly a cloaked form sprang down and grappled with him. Of all the times to run into a hostile muto, thought the Doctor despairingly. Enemies to everything but their own twisted and abandoned kind, the mutos attacked all strangers on sight. The Doctor disposed of his attacker fairly easily, but soon realised that he had more than one to deal with. More and more cloaked and hooded figures piled on top of him, and soon the Doctor was spread-eagled on his back in the mud, held powerless in the grip of many hands. One of the mutos, evidently a leader, looked round for some weapon to finish him. There was a jagged rock on the ground nearby. The muto lifted it up, raising it above his head with difficulty. He stood there, poised, ready to crash the rock down on the Doctor's head . . .

8

Captives of Davros

The Doctor struggled desperately to escape, but too many bodies were holding him down. Just as the rock seemed about to fall, a burly figure shoulder-charged the muto, sending him flying. The Doctor looked up into the face of Harry Sullivan! The jagged rock thudded into the mud close to the Doctor's head. Then a huge figure started plucking the other mutos from the Doctor, throwing them through the air in all directions.

Terrified by the sudden assault, the band of mutos scuttled off into the darkness. The next thing the Doctor knew, his two friends were helping him to his feet. The Doctor greeted them in astonished delight. 'Sarah! Harry! I don't believe it. I thought you'd been blown up in the Kaled City!'

'We never got there,' explained Sarah. 'Halfway across the Wastelands we were attacked by a band of wandering mutos. While we were fighting them off— the rocket blew up the Kaled city.'

'You could see the flames clear across the Wastelands,' Harry said. 'The poor old mutos were so scared they just ran for their lives.'

The Doctor shook his head wonderingly. 'Then what are you all doing here?'

Harry grinned. 'We knew you'd try to get back into the Bunker through the cave. We came to help.'

'Must you really go back?' Sarah asked.

'I must, Sarah. There's still a chance I'll manage to complete my mission. What's more, there's another very good reason.'

'To recover the Time Ring?'

'That bracelet the Time Lord gave me is our lifeline. Without it, we'll never get away from this planet.'

That was reason enough to convince even Sarah. They made their way out of the trench, across more Wastelands, until they reached the window in the rock wall through which they'd emerged earlier.

The Doctor moved aside the broken bars and helped Harry through. Sevrin was about to follow when the Doctor laid a hand on his arm. 'Will you do something for us, Sevrin—something important?'

'If I can,' Sevrin spoke in his deep, gentle voice.

'Over in the Thal city there's a girl called Bettan. She's trying to organise a resistance group. Will you round up any of your people who can fight, and join her? She's going to stage an attack on the main gate of the Bunker. The attack probably won't succeed, but it will keep the Elite troops occupied while I try to complete my mission.'

'Very well, Doctor. I will do what I can.'

Sarah took one of Sevrin's great hands in both of hers. 'Goodbye, Sevrin—and thank you.' The muto slipped away into the darkness. The Doctor helped Sarah through the gap and climbed through after her. Harry was waiting on the other side.

'We'd better stay close together, Sarah,' warned the Doctor. 'This cave is full of Davros's rejected experiments.'

Sarah shivered. 'Did you have to tell me that?'

Harry chuckled. 'Not scared, are you, Sarah?'

'Of course not!'

'Well you should be,' said the Doctor severely. 'One of them nearly had Harry for lunch!' With these consoling words the Doctor moved off into the darkness, Sarah and Harry following close behind.

The Doctor's Time Ring lay still unnoticed on Ronson's desk. No one was particularly interested in odds and ends taken from some mysterious alien, and the desk had been left undisturbed since its owner's death.

The plump communications scientist called Kavell was working at his own desk nearby when Gharman, Davros's chief assistant, came over to him. He cast a quick glance at the Elite guards on the door, and held up a piece of electronic circuitry. 'I'm having a problem with the dimensional thought circuit,' he said loudly. 'I wonder if you'd have a look at it.' Kavell looked up in surprise. The problem was completely out of his area. He was about to say so when Gharman whispered, 'Kavell—we've got to stop the Daleks!'

Kavell took the circuit and pretended to examine it. 'I want no part of it, Gharman. You saw what happened to Ronson. Davros will have us killed too, if he thinks we're plotting against him.'

'If we plan carefully he won't suspect.'

Kavell nodded towards the guard. 'What about the Elite Security Guards—they'll stay loyal to Davros.'

'That isn't important—not if the whole of the Scientific Corps turns against him. We can demand that the Dalek project is halted. Every day I become more convinced that this whole project is evil and immoral. These latest genetic changes——'

'What do you expect me to do?' whispered Kavell. He had no wish to prolong the conversation.

'Spread the word. Help me to convince the others that it's vital the whole Dalek project is ended.'

'I'll do what I can. I promise nothing——'

Kavell broke off short as Nyder came into the laboratory. Gharman snatched back his equipment and returned to his place. Kavell bent over his papers, working furiously.

Nyder seemed to have noticed nothing. He had a brief discussion about security matters with the guard on the door, then walked back to his own cubicle. As he sat behind his meticulously tidy desk, Nyder's mind was working furiously. He could very easily guess the kind of conversation Kavell and Gharman had been having. The only question in his mind was—what should he do about it?

Some time later, Nyder came back into the laboratory. Kavell was no longer there, but Gharman was still working at his desk. Nyder walked across to him. 'Gharman, I must talk to you. It's very important.'

Gharman didn't look up. 'You can see I'm busy . . .'

'Then soon,' insisted Nyder. 'Not here, somewhere private.'

Gharman looked up curiously. There was strain in Nyder's voice. 'What's all this about, Commander?'

Nyder seemed to be groping for words. 'Look, Gharman, you know me . . . I've served Davros faithfully for years, just as you have. I've never questioned anything he's done until now.'

'Go on,' said Gharman cautiously.

'He's become a megalomaniac. He's ready to sacrifice all of us just so his Dalek project can be completed.'

Gharman felt a sudden exultation. If even Nyder was coming round to his way of thinking . . . With him on their side victory was certain. 'Don't worry,

Commander,' he said reassuringly. 'You're not alone in your fears. Where can we talk safely?'

Nyder answered thoughtfully, 'There's the detention area on the lower level. Davros never goes there. We could use one of the cells.'

'Very well. I'll meet you down there as soon as I can.' Gharman bent over his papers, and Nyder walked quietly away.

Deep beneath the Bunker, Sarah held Harry's hand as she walked through the dank and dripping darkness of the caves. She kept her eyes tight shut most of the time. Various unpleasant hissings and gruntings came from all around, and Sarah had no wish to see what was making them. Harry's other hand was gripping the end of the Doctor's scarf, as the Doctor led them unerringly through the darkness. At least Harry *hoped* it was unerringly . . .

'Not much further,' whispered the Doctor. 'The entrance to the ventilation duct is just along here.'

Harry stopped and looked around. 'Are you *sure*, Doctor? I don't remember passing this little lot.' A colony of the giant clam creatures was clustered by the cave wall. They gave them a wide berth, but Harry couldn't resist giving the nearest one a passing kick—a gesture instantly regretted as the creature slid towards him, hissing loudly and jaws gaping wide.

Sarah screamed and backed away—straight towards the opening shell of another clam which gaped eagerly to receive her . . .

The Doctor pulled her to one side just as the clamshell clanged shut. Harry jumped away from his clam, and all three ran off into the darkness. The clams followed, hissing loudly, then suddenly subsided, waiting for another victim to pass by. Sarah shuddered. 'I'll never eat oysters again.'

'Lucky for us they're not very mobile,' said the Doctor. 'Maybe that's why Davros discarded them. Well—we've arrived.' He pointed to an opening in the cave wall—the other end of the ventilation duct.

Nervously Sarah said, 'Doctor, suppose there's something nasty waiting for us in there?'

'That's a thought,' the Doctor said cheerfully. 'Tell you what, we'll send Harry in first.'

Harry grinned, knowing full well that if the Doctor had suspected danger, he'd have gone in first himself. Harry crawled into the tunnel, then turned and helped Sarah to follow him. The Doctor took a last look round the cave and climbed after them. Harry in the lead, they began working their way down the narrow tunnel.

When Gharman reached the lower level, he found Nyder waiting for him. Without saying a word Nyder led the way through the detention area and into an empty cell.

In a low voice Gharman began, 'We'd better make this as quick as possible. We don't want to be missed.'

Nyder said, 'Tell me your plan.'

'Quite a number of scientists feel as we do. When we've collected enough support, we can give Davros an ultimatum.'

'What kind of ultimatum do you suggest?'

Gharman had worked it out in his mind. 'We shall only continue work on the Daleks if he restores *conscience* to the brain-pattern. The creatures *must* have a moral sense, the ability to judge between right and wrong . . . all the qualities that we believe essential in ourselves.'

Nyder nodded thoughtfully. 'And if he doesn't accept this ultimatum?'

'We will destroy all the work that has been done so far—everything! It will be as though the Daleks had never been created!'

'Excellent,' Nyder said crisply. 'I shall do my best to get some of the Security Corps on our side.' Casually he asked, 'Who can you count on among the scientists?'

Gharman considered. 'Kavell to begin with. Frenton, Parran, possibly Shonar . . .' He reeled off about a dozen names. 'All those have already been sounded out, and there are plenty of other likely ones we haven't spoken to as yet . . .'

'Thank you, Gharman. That is exactly what I needed to know.'

Gharman stared at him. There had been a sudden change in Nyder's tone. Then Gharman heard an all-too-familiar whirring sound. Davros was coming through the cell door, a squad of security men behind him. 'Davros will be most interested in your information,' added Nyder coldly.

Gharman stared round wildly. He was trapped in the little cell. There was nowhere to run. In a sudden frenzy he launched himself at Nyder, who sidestepped neatly and dropped him with one short chopping blow. Gharman collapsed in front of Davros's chair. Davros looked down at the sprawled body. 'A pity. He had a good scientific mind.'

Nyder drew his blaster. 'Shall I kill him?' he asked mildly.

'No. A little brain surgery will remove these stupid scruples, and we shall still have the benefit of his inventive skills.'

Nyder holstered his blaster regretfully. 'And the people he named?'

'The same for them.'

'I'll arrange for the arrests.'

'Not yet. We must move carefully. First we must learn exactly who are our allies, and who our enemies.'

Nyder snapped his fingers and a couple of security guards dragged Gharman away. Nyder was about to follow when he saw that Davros had not moved. 'What is it?'

'I heard something—in there.' Davros's withered hand gestured towards a tiny ventilation duct high in the cell wall.

Nyder could hear nothing. But he knew that Davros's electronically-boosted hearing was far better than his own. He put his ear close to the little grille. Was there something—a faint scuffling sound? 'I think there's someone in the ventilation system,' he whispered.

Harry pushed, aside the already-loosened hatch-cover and slithered out. 'Everything's quiet, Doctor,' he called, looking along the little tunnel. He helped Sarah out, and then the Doctor jumped down. Harry was just about to replace the hatch-cover when a dazzling spotlight illuminated the three of them. Behind it the Doctor could make out Davros, Nyder and a squad of black-uniformed security guards.

'Welcome back, Doctor,' said Davros.

The Doctor sighed, and turned to Sarah. 'There *was* something nasty waiting for us after all.'

The security squad marched the three captives to a room in the detention area. Various oddly-shaped pieces of electronic equipment lined the walls. There was something indescribably sinister about the place. The Doctor guessed the room was a kind of electronic interrogation chamber. Its equipment was designed to loosen the tongues of those unwilling to speak, and to check the truth of their stories.

The guards worked swiftly and efficiently. The Doctor was strapped into a metal chair, heavy straps holding his wrists and ankles. A metal helmet was lowered over the top of his head. He assumed that the contraption was some kind of lie-detector. What worried him far more was to see Sarah and Harry strapped to metal tables. These had clamps at each corner, holding the prisoners helpless. Electrodes were taped to their temples. Leads from the two tables were plugged into the control-console on the arm of Davros's chair.

Their work finished, the security men stood back. Davros wheeled his chair directly in front of the Doctor. Nyder, as always, was at his master's shoulder. There was a recording machine on Davros's other side.

Davros was leafing through a sheaf of computer print-outs. 'I have read the reports of your initial interrogation. The suggestion that you had travelled through Space and Time was rejected by the computer.'

The Doctor shrugged. 'Computers are limited. It had probably never been programmed for such a concept.'

'Such travel is beyond my scientific comprehension,' stated Davros. 'But not beyond my imagination. Why did you come here, from this future of yours?'

The Doctor saw no point in evasion. 'To stop the development of the Daleks. In what is to you the future, I have seen the carnage and destruction they will create.'

'So—my Daleks do survive?'

'As machines of war, weapons of hate.' The Doctor leaned forward, straining against his bonds in his urgency. 'There is still time to change that. You could make them a force for good in the Universe.'

'You have seen my Daleks in battle?' Davros demanded. 'Do they win? Do they always win?'

'They have been defeated many times—but never utterly. The Dalek menace always returns.'

'If they are the supreme war-machine, how *can* they lose?'

'Many reasons. Overwhelming opposition, poor information, simple misfortune . . .'

'You must tell me, Doctor. Where do the Daleks fail? What mistakes do they make?'

The Doctor shook his head. 'No, Davros. That is something the future must keep secret.'

Davros glided his wheelchair closer to the Doctor. 'You *will* tell me what I want to know because you have weaknesses. Ones that I have eliminated from myself, and from my Daleks. You are afflicted with a conscience, Doctor, and with compassion for others.'

The Doctor said nothing.

Davros went on remorselessly, 'Let me tell you what is going to happen, Doctor. You will answer all my questions, carefully and precisely. The instruments to which you are attached will instantly detect any attempt to lie.'

'And if I refuse to answer?'

'Your friends are attached to rather different instruments, Doctor.' Davros waved a hand towards Harry and Sarah. 'At the touch of a switch I can make them feel all the torments and agonies ever known.'

The Doctor's voice was hoarse with strain. 'If I tell you what you want to know, I betray the future. I can't do that.'

'You can and you will, Doctor,' said Davros gloatingly. 'You will tell me the reason for every Dalek defeat. With that knowledge I can programme my Daleks so there will be no errors, and no defeats. We shall change the future.'

The Doctor looked from Davros to Harry and Sarah. It was the most agonising decision he had ever faced. Davros was becoming impatient. 'Doctor! Either tell me about the Dalek future, or watch the suffering of your friends. Which is it to be?'

Slowly Davros moved his withered hand towards the switch . . .

Rebellion!

The Doctor knew he was beaten—at least for the time being. 'All right, Davros, all right. Just leave my friends alone.'

Davros kept his hand poised over the control. 'Then begin, Doctor.'

The Doctor paused, collecting his thoughts. In a flat, hopeless voice he began a catalogue of Dalek defeats, and the errors which had caused them. 'The Dalek invasion of Earth in the year Two Thousand was foiled because of an over-ambitious attempt to mine the core of the planet. The magnetic core of the planet was too strong, the human resistance too determined. On Mars the Daleks were finally defeated because of a virus which attacked the insulation cables of their electrical circuits. The Dalek war against the Venusian Colonies in the Space Year Seventeen Thousand was ended by the intervention of a rocket-fleet from the planet Hyperion . . .'

The Doctor's voice went on and on, every word recorded by the tape-recorder at Davros's elbow. Sarah and Harry listened in horror, relieved to have been spared the torments with which Davros had threatened them, realising how much it must cost the Doctor to place such priceless information in the hands of his enemy.

The Doctor talked till he was hoarse, dredging every possible scrap of Dalek history from his memory. At last his head slumped on his chest and he mumbled, 'That's all—all I can remember for now.' At the same moment the tape-machine clicked to a halt, its recording spool exhausted.

Davros nodded slowly. 'This seems an opportune moment to end this particular session. We can always resume later, under the same conditions. Commander Nyder, take the Doctor's two friends to the detention cell.'

Security guards unstrapped Sarah and Harry, lifted them down from the tables and dragged them away. The Doctor too was unstrapped from his chair. He slumped back exhausted. As the guards came to fetch him, Davros waved them away. 'I must thank you, Doctor. All this information will be programmed into the Dalek memory banks.' Davros slipped the tape-spool from the machine and handed it to Nyder. 'Commander, you will place this in the safe in my office. Its security is your personal responsibility. Remember, its value is beyond computation.' The Doctor's eyes followed the tape longingly as Nyder put it inside his tunic and left the room. He and Davros were alone now, though the Doctor guessed there would be more guards outside. He let himself slump deeper in the chair, doing his best to give the impression of utter defeat. But in his heart, or rather hearts, the Doctor was far from giving in. Characteristically, the Doctor wasted no time in regrets. He had given Davros the information he needed because there had been no alternative. He couldn't have allowed Sarah and Harry to suffer. What was done was done, the important thing now was to retrieve the situation.

With his enemy broken and defeated, Davros was in a relaxed, almost genial mood. 'Now, Doctor,' he said. 'Let us talk for a while, not as prisoner and captive, but as men of science. It is seldom that I meet someone whose intelligence even approaches my own . . .'

Sarah and Harry were marched along the corridor to a guarded cell and thrown inside. A tall, thin man in the uniform of one of Davros's Scientific Elite was stretched out on the bunk. He jumped to his feet and helped them to pick themselves up. 'Are you all right?' he asked anxiously.

'Just about,' said Sarah.

The man looked at Harry more closely. 'Forgive me, but aren't you one of the prisoners who escaped?'

Harry nodded. 'That's right. Who are you?'

'Until a little while ago I was a senior member of Davros's Scientific Elite. My name is Gharman.'

'And now you're a prisoner like us?' asked Sarah. 'What happened?'

Gharman told them of his attempt to rally the opposition to Davros, and his mistake in trusting Nyder. 'What's happening up there? I suppose the whole place is in an uproar.'

'We didn't get a chance to see very much,' said Harry. 'But as far as I could tell, everything seems to be running smoothly.'

Gharman began pacing about the cell. 'Yet Davros knows we're planning action against him. I should have expected mass arrests, executions . . .'

'Maybe that's too obvious for Davros?' suggested Sarah.

Gharman looked at her hopefully. 'He's being too clever for his own good. Every moment he delays our movement grows in strength. A *majority* of the scientists now want to end the Daleks. If they act now, they could break Davros's strength.' Gharman pounded his fist against the wall in an agony of frustration. 'If only I could get in touch with them.'

In the corridor outside, the plump little communications scientist, Kavell, was walking towards the cell door. The guard covered him with his rifle. 'Halt!'

Kavell glared back indignantly. 'I wish to question the prisoners.'

'No one may see the prisoners without a pass signed by Davros.'

'I'm aware of that. I have one here somewhere . . .' Kavell moved closer to the guard, his fingers reaching for the truncheon concealed inside his tunic . . .

Davros was still enjoying the spectacle of the Doctor's defeat. His prisoner's will seemed completely broken and he slumped dejectedly in his chair. 'I have committed the greatest act of treachery ever perpetrated,' groaned the Doctor. 'I have betrayed the unborn millions. Davros, I beg of you, stop the production of the Daleks.'

'Too late, Doctor. My automated workshops are already in full production of Dalek machines.'

'It isn't the machines that are evil, it's the minds of the creatures inside them. Minds that you created.'

'Evil?' said Davros thoughtfully. 'No, Doctor, I will not accept that. When all other life-forms are suppressed, when the Daleks are the supreme power of the Universe, then we shall have peace. All wars will end. The Daleks are the power not of evil but of good!'

The discussion seemed to revive the Doctor a little. He leaned forward in his chair. 'Evil that good may come, eh? Tell me, Davros, if you had created a virus in your laboratory, one that could destroy all life—would you use it?'

Davros seemed fascinated by the concept. 'To know that life and death on an enormous scale was within *my* choice . . . that the pressure of my thumb breaking the glass of a capsule could end everything . . . such power would set me among the Gods . . . yes, I would do it! And through the Daleks I shall have such power!'

The Doctor abandoned any faint hope he might have had of reasoning with Davros. He knew he was looking upon the face of utter madness. In one swift movement he sprang from his chair and grasped Davros's single wrist. 'Release me,' croaked the metallic voice.

The Doctor ignored him. With his free hand he reached for the row of controls on Davros's chair-arm. 'I imagine these switches control your life-support system. How long would you survive if I turned them off? Answer me, Davros!'

'Less than thirty seconds.'

The Doctor moved his hand closer to the switches. 'Order the complete close-down of the Dalek incubator section.'

'Destroy the Daleks? Never!'

With one sweep of his hand, the Doctor flicked an entire row of switches into the 'off' position. The body of Davros slumped forward, like a puppet whose strings have been cut. The Doctor waited a few seconds, then turned the switches on again. Eerily, Davros jerked back into life. When he was sure Davros could hear him the Doctor said, 'Next time I press those switches, they stay pressed. I mean it, Davros. Now—give the order!'

The lens in the centre of Davros's forehead seemed to glare at the Doctor. 'Even if I obey, there will be no escape for you.'

'That isn't important.'

Davros realised the Doctor was sincere. Tonelessly he said, 'Press the communicator switch—the red one at the end.' The Doctor did so. Leaning forward to a built-in microphone, Davros said, 'Davros to Elite Unit Seven. All survival maintenance systems are to be closed down. The Dalek creatures are to be destroyed.'

'Tell them the order is final and cannot be countermanded,' said the Doctor urgently. Davros hesitated. 'Tell them!' The Doctor's hand hovered over the switches.

Reluctantly Davros began, 'This order cannot . . .' Intent on his battle of wills with Davros, the Doctor realised too late that someone had entered the room. Nyder's truncheon took him across the back of the neck and he pitched to the floor. Again Davros leaned forward, almost gabbling in his haste. 'This is Davros. My last order is cancelled, repeat cancelled. No action is to be taken.' He sat back with a sigh of relief.

Nyder prodded the Doctor's body with the toe of one polished jackboot. 'What shall I do with him? It would be safest to kill him now.'

'Not yet. He still has knowledge that is vital to our future success. I shall wrench every last detail of it from his mind—and then he dies! Now, what of our rebellious scientists? How are they progressing?'

'Feeling against you is rising fast. Many of the Scientific Elite speak openly against you since the destruction of the city. Now some of the military are joining them.'

'It is as I expected.'

Nyder's face showed that he did not share his leader's calm. 'The rebels already outnumber those still loyal to you. Let me take a squad of Elite Guards to deal with them. I could wipe out their leaders in an hour.'

'You think like a soldier, Nyder. Rebellion is an idea. Suppress it too soon and it hides away and festers, bursting out elsewhere. My way is best.'

'As you wish.' Nyder hauled the semi-conscious Doctor to his feet. 'I'll take this one to the detention cell myself.' He kicked the Doctor brutally with his boot, 'Come on, you—move!' Nyder heaved the half-dazed Doctor to his feet and shoved him from the room.

Davros leaned towards his microphone. 'All Dalek Units. All Dalek Units. This is Davros . . .'

The Daleks swept through the burning Thal city killing all before them. As a party of them shot down some fleeing Thals another Dalek glided into sight.

'Davros has commanded all Dalek units to disengage and return to the Bunker immediately.'

'We obey.'

The Daleks spun round and glided towards the city gates.

Just outside the city, the girl Bettan and a ragged group of Thals crouched in a trench, watching their city burn. Bettan tensed, 'Quiet, there's something moving out there.'

The giant cloaked shape of a muto appeared over the edge of the trench. Bettan raised her rifle but a deep voice rumbled. 'No, do not shoot. I am a friend.'

The muto jumped into the trench, hands stretched out appealingly. 'You are the Thal girl called Bettan?'

'That's right. How did you know?'

'My name is Sevrin. The Doctor sent me to find you. He asked me to raise a band of my people to help you.'

'Well—where are they?'

Sevrin bowed his head. 'My people will not fight. The old hatreds are too deep.'

Bettan nodded, unsurprised. 'Then we'll have to manage alone.'

Sevrin looked at the tattered little group. They were a mixture of soldiers and civilians, clutching a motley assortment of weapons. 'This is all of you?'

'All I could find alive,' Bettan said simply. 'I covered most of the city. We managed to raid the armoury, though. We've got plenty of arms and ammunition.

Explosives too.' Sevrin saw that some of the Thals were clutching bombs and packs of explosives.

'You plan to attack the Bunker, with so few?' he asked doubtfully.

'Why not? At least we can die fighting.'

'Then I will help you,' Sevrin said determinedly. 'I am not afraid to fight.'

'Well, there's no point in delay.' Bettan began rousing her small group. 'Come on—it's time to move out!'

Nyder half-dragged, half-carried the semi-conscious Doctor towards the detention cell. He was pleased to see that the guard on the cell was alert. As soon as the guard saw Nyder approaching with his prisoner he turned to unlock the cell door. The door swung open and the guard turned round. Only then did Nyder realise that the 'guard' was Harry Sullivan.

Immediately Nyder threw the sagging Doctor at Harry and sprinted off down the corridor. Harry caught the Doctor, who was rapidly coming to, and led him into the cell. 'Things didn't go quite as planned,' he said apologetically.

Shaking his head to clear it, the Doctor saw that the cell held Sarah and two members of Davros's Scientific Elite. On the bunk was a guard, stripped of his uniform and bound and gagged with torn-up blankets.

Sarah helped the Doctor to sit down. 'He's still a bit groggy,' Harry said.

Sarah saw the Doctor looking at the two scientists. 'They're called Kavell and Gharman,' she explained. 'Kavell helped us escape. He and Gharman are leading the opposition to Davros.'

Gharman started to leave the cell. 'Come on, Kavell, we've a lot to do. We must act quickly . . .'

'Wait,' said the Doctor. 'I think Davros knows about you. Just as I was coming to, I heard him talking to Nyder.'

'Then why hasn't he taken more action against us?'

'Perhaps he doesn't care?' suggested Kavell. Knocking out the guard had given him new confidence. 'Davros knows we are too many for him.'

The Doctor shook his head, then winced as a stab of pain shot through him. 'I think he has some trap ready for you. Be careful.'

Gharman too seemed to be filled with confidence. 'Thanks for the warning, Doctor, I think we can take care of Davros.'

'That's right,' agreed Kavell. 'We're too many for him now.'

Eagerly the two scientists bustled out of the cell, hurrying off to rally their fellow conspirators.

The Doctor sat for a moment, head in his hands. He was summoning all the powers of his resilient Time Lord body to overcome the effects of his recent blow. Suddenly he rose and stretched, apparently as good as new. Sarah looked dubiously at him. 'I suppose it's no good telling you to rest for a while?'

'No, it isn't. For one thing this place isn't safe. For another, there's too much to be done. First, we've got to recover that Time Ring. Remember, we'll never get off this planet without it. Second, I *must* find and destroy that tape Davros made. The knowledge it holds could make the Daleks totally invincible.'

Full of his old determination, the Doctor led Harry and Sarah from the cell.

Outside the Bunker armoury, two of Nyder's Security Elite stood on watch, immaculate in their black uniforms. A head popped round the corner of a nearby corridor, and then popped back. It was Gharman, three more scientists behind him. 'Now remember,' he whispered, 'we resort to violence *only* if there is no other way.'

Chatting idly among themselves, the scientists strolled round the corner. The guards paid no particular attention as they drew level. Suddenly Gharman drew a hidden pistol and jammed it into the nearest guard's ribs. The second guard reacted instantly. Grabbing the nearest scientist as a shield, he hurled him into Gharman, who was knocked to the floor. Raising his rifle, the guard shot down another scientist, then crumpled and fell himself as Gharman fired from the floor. By now the third scientist had produced a gun, and disarmed the remaining guard. Gharman got to his feet, looking at the two bodies. 'A stupid waste of life,' he said sadly.

'Our intention is to make a bloodless revolution.' He waved towards the captured guard. 'Take him away and lock him up with the others. Get his keys first.'

Gharman unlocked the armoury door and they went inside. The plain metal room was lined with racks of weapons, and shelves holding detonators and explosives. Gharman turned to the scientist. 'Take as many weapons as you can carry and pass them out to our people.' At that moment Kavell hurried into the armoury.

'Well done, Gharman!' Before Gharman could reply the little man went on excitedly, 'They're coming over to our side in droves. Security Guards too. We have the backing of at least eighty per cent of those in the Bunker. We're winning, Gharman, we're winning . . .'

Gharman took a rifle from the rack and passed it to Kavell. He took another for himself. Holding the unaccustomed weapon awkwardly, he made for the door. 'Very well,' he said. 'Let's finish it off . . .'

In the huge emptiness of the main laboratory, Davros sat alone in his chair. From the corridors all round, he heard the sounds of shooting, the bustle of running feet, even the occasional burst of cheering. Davros showed no reaction. He just sat there, silently, waiting, a faint smile on the thin, lipless mouth . . . Slowly the fingers of his one withered hand began drumming on the arm of the chair.

10

Decision for the Doctor

Nyder ran into the laboratory, blaster in hand. His uniform was dishevelled, and his usual cold manner replaced by an air of terror. 'Davros, they're taking over. Soon they'll be in total control. *Everyone's* turned against us, even men I thought I could trust . . .'

Davros didn't answer. The only sound was the drumming of his fingers.

Nyder's voice rose in panic. 'Listen, I've got a squad of men in section nine. If I order them into action now, they might stay loyal. Davros . . .'

The metallic voice was so quiet as to be almost inaudible. 'I hear you, Nyder.'

'Then tell me what to do!' Nyder had grown so used to the support of Davros that without it he felt lost and abandoned.

'Find their leaders. Hand over your weapons to them. Order all members of your Security Guard to do the same. Tell the rebel leaders that *I* have given these orders to avoid bloodshed. Tell them I will submit to their demands.'

Nyder shook his head incredulously. 'We admit we're beaten? We simply surrender?'

'That is what they will believe.'

The evasiveness of this answer gave Nyder new hope. 'You mean to——'

Davros interrupted him. 'Nyder! You—and the rebels—will find out what I mean in good time. Now—carry out my orders.'

The route followed by the Doctor and his friends took them past the armoury. The doors gaped open, and Harry couldn't resist taking a look inside. 'Hang on, Doctor. This might come in handy.'

They followed him into the armoury. There were still plenty of weapons on the shelves. Harry grabbed a rifle for himself and offered one to the Doctor. The Doctor shook his head absentmindedly and began hunting around the wall cupboards. Sarah saw that he was filling his pockets with small waxed cartons, spools of wire, and a variety of other objects. 'That's explosive, isn't it, Doctor?' she asked.

'Explosives and detonators,' agreed the Doctor. 'Seems almost providential.'

'What are you going to use it for?'

The Doctor sighed. 'The Time Lords gave me three options. Discover the Daleks' weakness—if they have one. Alter their genetic development, so they become less evil. Or destroy them entirely. Now only the last option is still open.' As the Doctor looked down at her, Sarah was surprised to see the sadness in his eyes. 'I'm going to kill everything in that incubator room. I'm going to destroy the Daleks for ever.'

Davros sat silently in the empty laboratory. Nyder entered, still under strain, but calmer now. 'Everything has been done as you ordered. They are on their way.'

Davros nodded, but said nothing. Nyder took up his usual position behind Davros's chair. A few minutes later Kavell and Gharman entered. They made a strangely incongruous picture, one short and plump, the other tall and thin. Davros spoke, 'You have something to say to me?'

Hesitantly Gharman stepped forward. He knew that he had won, that Davros was in his power, yet the habit of years made his voice respectful. 'Davros, no one questions that under your guidance we have made incredible progress . . .'

Ruthlessly Davros interrupted. 'You did not come here to flatter me. You came to deliver an ultimatum. Do so.'

'Very well. Initially the Dalek was intended as a life-support system for the creature into which we Kaleds must ultimately evolve. However we feel the concept has been perverted. You have tampered with the genetic structure of your forced mutations to create a ruthless power for evil. This must not continue.'

'What do you suggest?'

'All work on the Daleks will cease immediately. Those created so far will be destroyed. If you agree to these terms we shall be proud to work under your guidance on the rebuilding of our society.'

'And if I refuse?'

Gharman's voice hardened. 'The Daleks will still be destroyed. You will be imprisoned, and we shall continue under a democratically elected leader.' Davros was silent. After a moment Gharman said nervously, 'Well?'

'At least do me the courtesy of allowing me time to consider.' Davros spun his chair and wheeled it to the other end of the laboratory. Gharman and Kavell looked nervously at each other, wondering how they had lost the initiative. After a long and agonising pause, Davros wheeled his chair back to them. 'I have made my decision. I will accept your ultimatum—on condition that I am first allowed to speak to a full meeting of the Elite, both Scientific and Security. When I have finished, a vote will be taken. I will abide by the decision of the majority.' Taken aback, the two delegates said nothing. 'Well?' snapped Davros. 'Do you agree? You wish to be "democratic", do you not?'

Gharman looked at Kavell, who shrugged. Both knew that ninety per cent of those in the Bunker were now against Davros. What harm could it do to let a once-honoured leader save his face? 'Very well,' Gharman said. 'It is agreed.'

Davros retained control till the last. 'The meeting will take place immediately. Arrange it. You may go now.' Dismissed, Gharman and Kavell turned and left. Once they were out of the room, Davros spun his chair to face Nyder. There was fierce exultation in the metallic voice. 'Victory is ours, Nyder. Democracy, freedom, fairness . . .' Davros spat out the words like oaths. 'Achievement comes through power, and power through strength. *They have lost!*'

Concealed in a trench near to the Bunker, Bettan and her small force crouched in hiding. Outside the trench a long line of Daleks was sweeping past. Bettan looked up as they disappeared from sight. 'The blockhouse is just over the next rise. That's where they must be heading.'

Sevrin tapped her on the shoulder. 'Keep down. There are more coming.'

Another line of Daleks glided by. When they were gone Sevrin said, 'Will you still attack the Bunker now the Daleks are back?'

Bettan nodded slowly. 'Why not? Davros and his Daleks will soon be inside the Bunker together. We're going to make sure they stay there—for ever!'

*

The Doctor, Harry and Sarah stood outside the heavy door with its glass viewing panel—the door to which Ronson had earlier brought the Doctor. The Doctor slid back the panel-cover and a greenish light spilled over his face. 'Are there really Daleks in there?' asked Sarah.

'The flesh and blood part of them—if indeed it is still flesh and blood after Davros's genetic tampering.' He began busying himself with detonators, explosives and coils of wire. Harry plucked up courage and looked through the panel.

Morbid curiosity made Sarah ask, 'What do they look like?'

Harry peered into the dim light. 'They seem to be in different stages of development. Some are in jars and tanks . . . others seem to be able to move around. Maybe they're fully grown ones . . .'

The Doctor, his preparations completed, passed Harry a large spool of wire. 'Pay this out to me slowly, will you?' He put his hand on the door.

'You're not going in there, Doctor?' asked Sarah.

'Only for a moment—the creatures are harmless—I think. Just rather unpleasant . . .'

Harry braced himself. 'Do you want me to come in with you?'

To his relief the Doctor said, 'No need, Harry. It's just a matter of setting the charges where they'll do most damage. Shouldn't take long.' Unwinding wire from Harry's spool as he went along, the Doctor disappeared inside the Incubator Room.

After a time the tugging on the spool stopped. Evidently the Doctor had all the wire he needed. Nothing happened for quite a while. All they could do was wait.

Inside the Incubator Room, the Doctor bent his head over his work, paying no attention to the horrors all around him. Greenish light from the tanks filled the room. Inside those tanks ghastly-shaped creatures twisted and writhed in agitation, while in the darker corners of the room other monstrosities cowered away timidly. The Doctor moved from place to place, planting packets of explosives, connecting his central wire to the terminal on each packet. He didn't notice that out of the darkness something shapeless was oozing across the floor towards him . . .

In the corridor Sarah looked worriedly at Harry. 'What's taking him so long?'

'It's a pretty delicate job, planting explosives.'

'Well he *should* be finished by now. I'm going to take a look.' A choking cry from inside the room sent them running through the door. In the dim green light, they could see the Doctor swaying wildly. Something like a coating of live black tar was covering his legs, flowing steadily upwards as if to engulf him . . .

'Harry, help me,' yelled Sarah. She dashed into the room and grabbed one of the Doctor's arms. Harry grabbed the other, and they heaved him free of the pool of black liquid, which let go its grip with an ugly squelching sound. All three stumbled out of the room, and Harry slammed the door behind them.

Sarah shuddered. 'What was that awful stuff?'

'Some kind of nutrient, I think. Seemed almost alive, didn't it?' The Doctor had held on to the wire which was now running under the door. For want of a knife, he bit through the wire with his teeth and began peeling back the protective plastic coating, revealing the gleaming metal underneath. Then he peeled off another length of wire, bared both ends and looked round for a power-source. A wall-light glowed dimly nearby. In a moment the Doctor had dismantled it, and fixed one end of his wire to its inner workings, sucking his fingers as blue sparks shot out. Holding the wire from the light in one hand, the wire from under the door in the other, the Doctor said, 'All I have to do is touch *this* wire to this one, and the explosives will go off.'

Sarah spoke impatiently, 'Then what are you waiting for?'

'Do I have the right?' said the Doctor simply.

Sarah was astonished. 'To destroy the Daleks? How can you possibly doubt it? You know what they'll become.'

In an agonised voice the Doctor tried to explain, 'It isn't so simple, Sarah. The evil of the Daleks produced counter-reactions of good. Many future worlds will stop warring among themselves, join in alliance to fight the Daleks.' Sarah looked at him, unable to believe that the Doctor was held up by ethical scruples at a time like this. But the Doctor was perfectly serious. To him the moral issue was real and vital. 'Suppose somebody who knew the future told you a certain child would grow up to be an evil dictator—could you then destroy that child?'

Sarah made a last attempt to talk sense into him. 'We're not talking about some imaginary child, Doctor, we're talking about the Daleks. The most evil creatures ever created. Complete your mission and destroy them. You must!'

The Doctor stared at the gleaming wires as though mesmerised. 'I simply have to touch *this* to *this* and generations of people might live without fear, never even hearing the word "Dalek".'

'Then do it,' urged Sarah. 'Suppose it was a question of wiping out the bacteria that caused some terrible disease. You wouldn't hesitate then, would you?'

The Doctor looked at her solemnly. 'But if I wipe out a whole intelligent life-form, I'll be no better than the Daleks myself.' In an agony of indecision, the Doctor repeated his question. 'I could destroy the Daleks, here and now. But do I have the right?'

11

Triumph of the Daleks

They were never to know how the Doctor would have resolved his moral dilemma. A shout from the other end of the corridor interrupted them. They turned to see Gharman running towards them his face alight with triumph. 'Doctor, I've been looking for you. We've won! Davros has submitted to all our terms!'

'Davros surrendered? Just like that?'

Gharman waved a dismissive hand. 'He is trying to save face, of course. He asked to be allowed to speak to a full meeting of the Elite. But that's no more than a formality. The voting will be a landslide against him.'

The Doctor took the wire projecting beneath the door and gave a sudden heave. Somewhere inside the room the wire snapped. The Doctor reeled it in until the broken end came from under the door. 'Gharman, I'm more grateful than you'll ever know. You've saved me from the most terrible decision of my life.'

Gharman was too excited to listen to him. 'The meeting is just about to begin, Doctor. I wanted you to be there. Will you come?' Taking the Doctor's assent for granted, he led the way back down the corridor.

'With the greatest of pleasure.'

The Doctor followed the eager Gharman, and Sarah and Harry hurried after them. At the back of her mind, Sarah was wishing Gharman had arrived a moment later. The Doctor might have decided to set off those explosives after all . . .

The big central laboratory was an impressive sight. Every scientist and security man in the Bunker had somehow managed to squeeze inside. They were all tightly packed on one side of the room. On the other Davros sat alone in his chair, Nyder by his side. The Doctor, Harry and Sarah watched from a position by one of the doors. Gharman stood at the front of the crowd, opposite Davros. 'Everyone is here, Davros,' he said. 'We are waiting to hear whatever you have to say.'

Davros began to speak. He described his years of struggle to develop the travel machine that would protect the creatures into which their race must evolve, of his desire that when the war was over, his own race should stand supreme. The assembled crowd listened in courteous silence, but it was clear that his words had no appeal for them. At long last the Kaleds were sickened of war and slaughter. They wanted no part of Davros's dreams of conquest.

Satisfied that the vote against Davros would indeed be a landslide, the Doctor whispered to Sarah and Harry, 'Let's get the Time Ring while they're all occupied.'

They began working their way round the edge of the crowd towards the corner desk that had once been Ronson's. Progress was slow, since the crowd was densely packed. All the while they heard Davros droning on. By now the crowd was shuffling restlessly, impatient for him to end. 'At this very moment,' Davros was saying, 'the production lines stand ready in the workshops, on the lower levels. They are totally automated, fully programmed. The Daleks no longer depend on us— they are a power in their own right. Would you end everything we have achieved together?'

The Doctor and his friends reached Ronson's desk at last. The Doctor's possessions were still strewn on top of it, and he began stuffing them back in his pocket. But there was no sign of the Time Ring! Frantically they began to search.

Davros had wheeled his chair over to a control panel set into one wall, the crowd falling back before him. He pointed his withered hand at a large red button. 'This is a destruct button. Press it and you will destroy everything in the Bunker, outside of this room. You will destroy the Daleks, and with them the future of our race. Which of you will do it?' The crowd shuffled uneasily. Such was the dominance of Davros's personality that no one dared step forward. 'You are men without courage,' Davros spoke scornfully. 'You have lost the right to survive.'

Stung by the contempt in his voice, Gharman stepped forward to address the crowd. 'You have heard Davros's case. What he does not tell you is that there *is* another way—to destroy his conditioned, conscienceless creatures and allow our mutation to follow its natural course. Our race will survive—survive with all the strengths and weaknesses we have ourselves, not as an unfeeling and heartless monstrosity. That is our choice. Now it is time to decide.'

Most of this debate was lost on the Doctor and his friends, since they were frantically searching the area round the desk. It was Sarah who spotted the Time Ring at last. It had fallen from the desk and had been kicked by some careless foot until it was almost out of sight beneath a work-bench. Sarah wriggled underneath, scooped out the bracelet and handed it to the Doctor, who slipped it back on his arm with a sigh of relief. 'Bless you, Sarah. Now if we can only manage to find that tape-recording and destroy it—we can all go home!'

Over the heads of the crowd they heard once more the voice of Davros. 'You have heard my case, and you have heard Gharman's. I will give you a few more minutes to decide. Then you must answer, not only to me, but to your future.'

Outside the blockhouse that led to the Bunker a small army of Daleks was grouped, silently waiting. Hidden in a trench nearby, Bettan, Sevrin and their little band looked on, wondering what was happening.

(In the centre of the laboratory, isolated amidst a largely-hostile crowd, Davros was also waiting. He glanced at a digital clock set in one wall. As the figures clicked up to record the passing of another time-unit, his finger stabbed down on one of the buttons on his console.)

The metal gates of the blockhouse slid smoothly open.

Bettan and Sevrin watched as the army of Daleks glided through. The inner gates opened, and the Daleks disappeared down the tunnel that led to the Bunker. No sooner were they out of sight than Bettan and her ragged band of commandos ran through the gates after them.

Bettan gave swift orders. 'Right. Set charges there . . . there, and more there. Go as deep inside the tunnel as you can without being seen.' She turned to Sevrin. 'This is the only way into the Bunker?'

'It is now,' Sevrin said grimly. 'There was once a way in from the Kaled City, but your rocket buried that for ever.'

Bettan nodded satisfied. 'Then if we do the same to *this* entrance, we can bury the Daleks with those who created them.' There was no pity in her voice. The slaughter and destruction she had seen in her own city were too fresh in her mind.

'But surely you will give the Doctor and his friends time to get clear?'

Bettan shook her head. 'I can't. I *must* blow the tunnel as soon as the charges are prepared. If anyone sees what we're doing, we're too few to fight them off.'

'How long?' asked Sevrin.

'Thirty minutes. Possibly less.'

'Then I must go inside and warn the Doctor.'

'That's very brave of you,' said Bettan. She hesitated. 'You understand, I *can't* delay things? If you're not back by the time we're ready . . .'

'I understand,' said Sevrin. 'But I must try.'

Bettan nodded. 'Good luck. I hope you make it.' It was clear that she never expected to see him again. Swiftly and silently, Sevrin ran down the tunnel into the Bunker.

Sarah, Harry and the Doctor were waiting impatiently. 'How much longer?' asked Sarah.

'Not long,' whispered the Doctor. 'It's nearly time for the grand finale.' As yet he didn't realise the ghastly truth of his words.

Davros wheeled his chair to face the crowd. 'You have had ample time to decide. Let all those who are loyal to me and to the future of our race move forward to stand at my side.' The gap between Davros and the crowd seemed very large now. At first no one moved to cross it. At last one man moved. Then another. A handful more, and that was all. Davros looked round. 'No more?' he asked ironically. 'Kravos, will you betray me? Fenatin—my science saved your life. Do *you* turn against me?' The named men shuffled uneasily. But they did not move to join him.

The Doctor watched, almost with pity, as Davros appealed in vain to first one man then another. It was somehow degrading to see him plead. Why didn't he just accept defeat?

Harry noticed that Nyder had edged away from Davros and was slipping out of the laboratory. He nudged the Doctor. 'Where do you think old Nyder's off to?'

The Doctor gave him a thoughtful look. A strong feeling of unease was creeping over him. Something about Davros's behaviour just didn't ring true, and Nyder's disappearing act made the feeling stronger. 'Let's find out,' he suggested. They slipped out of the laboratory after Nyder.

They followed him down one of the perimeter corridors that ran round the laboratory and up some steps, catching up with him along an upper corridor. At the sight of his unwelcome followers Nyder reached for a gun, but Harry tackled him hard, and sent him crashing half-stunned to the ground.

Nyder scrambled to his feet and started to run, but the Doctor reached out a long arm to grab him. Harry joined in and there was a wild three-cornered fight which ended with Nyder disarmed and subdued. 'Now, where were you off to in such a hurry?' panted the Doctor.

Nyder shrugged. 'I was getting out while I could. Davros is finished—that means I'm finished too.'

The Doctor shook his head. 'That doesn't ring quite true. Let's try something else. Where's Davros's office? I want the tape-recording you took away.'

Nyder said nothing. Harry grabbed him by the throat and shook him till he choked. 'Just along there . . .' Nyder nodded to a heavy steel door along the corridor. They moved to the door. It was locked. Nyder produced a key to open it and they all went inside.

Davros's office was small and functional, the walls covered with blueprints of early Dalek designs. The main feature was a small inner window which looked down on to the main laboratory below. They could see Davros haranguing the crowd, still with only one or two supporters beside him. The Doctor looked at Nyder. 'Where is it?' he snapped. Nyder said nothing, but instinctively his eyes flickered to a safe set in the wall. There was a combination-dial in the door. 'Be a good chap and open it for us,' urged the Doctor.

'Only Davros knows the combination.'

The Doctor looked at the safe. It was set fairly high in the wall. He pushed a chair underneath and sat down. 'I doubt that. Davros has the use of only one arm.' The Doctor raised his own right arm. From a sitting position the safe dial was well out of reach. 'You must have to open the safe for him. So open it for us, Nyder, or I'll let Harry throttle you. We're desperate men, remember.' Harry did his best to look ferocious. He must have done pretty well. Nyder went to the safe and spun the dials. The door swung open, revealing the tape-spool on a shelf in plain sight. The Doctor took it out and dropped it into a metal waste-bin. 'Now, we need some way to destroy it.'

'How about this, Doctor?' Harry had picked up a Dalek gun from the desk. Evidently an experimental model it was plugged into a portable power pack.

'A Dalek gun,' said the Doctor, pleased. 'How *very* fitting!' With an appropriately ceremonial air, he raised the gun and fired it. The spool exploded into flames. They stood and watched it burn. Unfortunately they forgot to watch Nyder at the same time. Seizing his chance, he sprinted through the door, slamming and locking it behind him. Harry rattled the door furiously but it was no use. The Doctor was quite unconcerned. 'Let him go, Harry, he's not important. Our job here's over now anyway. The power of Davros has been broken. Old Gharman will see that the Daleks of the future are, well, humanised, you might say.'

'What about the ones Davros already has operational, Doctor?' Sarah asked. 'The ones you saw attacking the Thal City.'

'Gharman will have them recalled and destroyed,' said the Doctor reassuringly.

Harry thumped the door. 'Well, we're still locked in.'

The Doctor smiled. 'Doesn't matter in the least, old chap. We'll simply leave from here. All we have to do is stand in a circle and touch the Time Ring . . .' The Doctor touched his wrist. 'Oh no!' The Time Ring wasn't there.

They stared wildly at each other. 'It's outside,' said Sarah suddenly. 'It's got to be. It must have come off in that fight with Nyder.'

Suddenly getting the door open became a matter of vital importance. Harry and the Doctor kicked at it to no avail. They tried the Dalek gun on it, but the power-pack must have been nearly exhausted. After charring the steel quite promisingly, the gun suddenly went dead. The Doctor produced a piece of wire and tried to pick the lock. 'It's no good,' he said disgustedly. 'He's left the key in the lock on the other side. Oh well, never mind. When the dethroning of Davros is over I expect someone will turn up to let us out.' The Doctor wandered over and looked at the scene in the laboratory below them. 'You know,' he said slowly. 'I *still* can't help feeling it's unlike Davros to give in so easily.'

The Doctor noticed a switch near a speaker-grille beside the window. He flicked it idly. Immediately they could hear the voice of Davros in the laboratory below. Isolated and alone, he was still talking as if *he* was the one who held power. 'This is your last chance. Join me, or suffer the consequences!' No one moved.

Pityingly Gharman said, 'Accept defeat. It is over for you, Davros!'

'No!' shouted Davros suddenly. 'It is over for *you*! I allowed this charade for only one reason. I wanted to know who was truly loyal to me.' He gestured at the small group around him. 'With these few faithful helpers, I shall continue my great work.'

From his viewpoint above the laboratory, the Doctor saw Gharman's shake of the head. 'You are insane to talk like this, you must see that you are totally outnumbered.'

'No,' said Davros again, this time his voice low and menacing. 'It is *you* who are outnumbered, Gharman, you and your traitor friends.' With an elaborate gesture, Davros pressed a control. Every one of the many doors around the laboratory slid open. Framed in each stood a Dalek.

The crowd fell back in terror as the Daleks glided into the room.

12

A Kind of Victory

Davros and his supporters retreated into one corner of the room. The rest, the vast majority, were herded into a tightly packed circle, surrounded by a ring of Daleks. Tighter and tighter the circle was drawn until men were jammed one against the other. For a long, terrible moment Davros regarded his enemies. Then he said, 'Exterminate them!' Fire blazed from the Dalek guns.

The Doctor and his horrified friends had grandstand seats at a massacre. Bodies fell in swathes as the Daleks fired into the tightly packed crowd, and the room was full of screaming. Nyder entered from a door by Davros's side, and stood looking on with evident satisfaction. Not all of Davros's supporters were so lacking in feeling. One of them, an officer of the Security Elite, recoiled in horror from the carnage. 'Stop them, Davros,' he screamed, 'you've *got* to stop them.' He grabbed Davros by the shoulder, but Nyder pulled him back, shoving him out into the crowd. Away from the charmed group around Davros, he was immediately shot down by Dalek guns.

Sarah turned sickened from the slaughter below and hammered hysterically on the door. 'Let us out. Please someone let us out!' she screamed.

Harry tried to calm her. 'It's no use, Sarah . . .'

The Doctor tapped him on the shoulder. 'Don't be so sure, Harry!' He pointed. The handle of the door was moving, turned from the outside. They heard the key in the lock. The door began opening slowly, and a gun-muzzle appeared. The Doctor and Harry backed away—and Sevrin's hooded face appeared round the door.

Sarah ran to him and hugged him, but he cut short her thanks. 'I was looking for you when I heard your voice. We have very little time. The Thals have set explosive charges at the entrance. They'll detonate as soon as they're ready.'

'Thank you, Sevrin,' said the Doctor. 'Now if I can just find that Time Ring . . .'

They found the Time Ring easily enough, in the corridor outside. Just as the Doctor snatched it up, a Dalek appeared at the end of the corridor. They set off at a run, only to find a second Dalek facing them at the other end. Skidding round they hurled themselves down a side corridor, relieved to see no more Daleks. They ran frantically down endless corridors, not pausing till the Daleks were far behind. The Doctor stopped in a wide corridor, buttressed by huge pillars. 'We are near the entrance now,' gasped Sevrin. 'If we can make it through the next section we'll be safe.'

The Doctor slipped the Time Ring from his wrist and passed it to Sarah. 'Look after this for me, will you? Sevrin—I'm relying on you to get my friends out of here.'

Sarah stared at him. 'What are you going to do?'

'I'm going back to the Incubator Room. The charges are still laid. This time I'll blow the place up as I should have done before. Now, you three get out of here.'

Before anyone could argue the Doctor was sprinting down one of the side corridors. 'Come,' Sevrin spoke urgently. 'Time is short now.' Quickly he led them on their way.

Davros regarded the bodies of his fallen enemies. 'Now the traitors have been disposed of, the Daleks will take over security of the Bunker. The rest of us will go on, working to improve every aspect of Dalek design.'

Nyder ran back into the laboratory, stepping casually over the fallen bodies. 'Davros, the alien prisoners I locked in your office have escaped.' Davros could not bear that anything should mar his triumph.

'Then they must be found. Seek them out and exterminate them.'

Immediately there came a chorus of Dalek voices, 'We obey!' Daleks glided from the laboratory.

*

Bettan stood waiting in the blockhouse, looking nervously down the tunnel. A Thal soldier came running out of the tunnel, playing out flex behind him. He ran up to Bettan. 'That's the last charge in position.'

'Very well, prepare to detonate.'

The soldier began wiring the flex to a big portable field-detonator. Bettan stood watching him, spinning round as she heard footsteps running out of the tunnel. It was Sevrin with Harry and Sarah. 'I'd given you up,' she said, amazed. 'Better move back, we're almost ready to detonate.'

Sarah clutched her arm. 'You *can't*, not yet. The Doctor's still inside . . .'

Harry added his plea. 'Give him a few minutes more at least.'

Bettan hesitated. 'Very well, just a few minutes. But if the Daleks start coming up that tunnel—then I detonate!'

The Doctor crouched in the Incubator Room, rewiring the charges with nimble fingers, ignoring once more the horrors gibbering all around him. His work concluded, he backed out into the corridor, trailing the wire behind him. The wire from the wall power-source was still stretched from the other side of the corridor. The Doctor grabbed it and was just about to bring the two wires together when a Dalek appeared at the end of the corridor. It fired, charring the wall by the Doctor's head. The Doctor leaped back, letting go of both wires as he did so. He sheltered behind the wall buttress and peered out. The Dalek hadn't moved. The Doctor could see the ends of the two wires, tantalisingly close together. If he could only manage to join them . . . He stretched out a long arm, grabbed the nearest wire, and started edging it towards the other. The Dalek spotted the movement and fired again. The edge of its blast caught the tip of the Doctor's fingers and he snatched his hand back in pain.

A wild thought struck the Doctor. He looked at the end of the two wires, so very near each other . . . It might work, he thought. Suddenly the Doctor leaped from cover and zig-zagged down the corridor in full view of the Dalek. It fired, missed, fired again. The second blast missed too, and the Doctor leaped into a side-corridor out of sight. Angrily the Dalek started in pursuit. As it glided down the corridor the metal of its body casing, vibrant with static electricity, passed over the two wires and completed the circuit . . . There was a huge detonation and the wall of the Incubator Room exploded outwards, burying the Dalek in rubble. The Doctor popped his head round the corner, took a quick look at the wreckage. He gave a satisfied nod and started sprinting for the main exit.

In the blockhouse checkpoint, the anxious group looked down the empty tunnel. Nervously one of the soldiers began fiddling with the scanning equipment. Suddenly he shouted, 'Look, I'm getting a picture on one of these scanners.' Sure enough, one of the screens was showing a blurred picture of the main laboratory. They could even hear a faint murmur of sound.

'Try for more volume,' ordered Bettan. 'We may be able to find out what's happening down there.'

Obediently the soldier adjusted controls. The picture improved, and sound came through clearly. Sarah shivered as she heard the voice of Davros. 'Send a patrol of Daleks to secure the main entrance.'

'I obey.'

'That is *it*,' snapped Bettan. 'I *must* detonate right away.'

'Give it one minute more,' begged Harry, 'Please!'

Bettan said, 'I'm sorry. I daren't wait any longer.' She turned to the soldier. 'Get those tunnel doors closed and we'll detonate from in here.'

The Doctor was haring down a corridor, running for his life. A patrol of Daleks appeared behind him. Their guns blazed and their metallic voices filled the air. 'Exterminate! Exterminate! Exterminate!'

Safe in his laboratory, surrounded by a guard of Daleks, Davros was preparing to resume work. His eye was caught by flashing lights on an indicator panel. He wheeled his chair round angrily. 'The Dalek production line has been started. I gave no such order. Who is responsible?'

Davros looked angrily at the handful of surviving scientists scattered about the room. None of them spoke. A Dalek glided forward. 'I gave the order,' said the metallic voice.

Davros looked at his creation angrily. Some minor malfunction, no doubt. It could be corrected, perhaps even by a simple verbal re-programming. He glided his chair up to the Dalek and spoke slowly and clearly. 'You will perform no function unless directly ordered by *me*. You will obey only *my* commands. The Dalek production line will be halted immediately.'

The Dalek did not move.

Davros was enraged. 'You heard my order. Obey! Obey!'

Still the Dalek did not move. Nyder sighed. He moved towards the control panel. 'All right, I'll do it . . .' He reached for the control. Almost casually, the nearest Dalek swivelled round and blasted him down. Davros looked on unbelievingly as Nyder's smoking body twisted and fell.

The Dalek spoke again, 'Production will continue.' Davros backed his chair slowly away . . .

Harry and Sarah watched helplessly as the iron doors of the tunnel began to slide slowly closed. Bettan stood watching too, beside her a soldier with his hand on the plunger of an old-fashioned field detonator. Bettan said, 'Fire!'

The soldier heaved up the plunger handle. He was about to force it down, when Sarah screamed, 'Wait, please wait. The Doctor's coming!'

The soldier hesitated. Harry and Sarah ran to the doors and held them back by force. The Doctor came tearing along the tunnel, a patrol of Daleks close behind him. Just as their strength failed, the Doctor reached the fast-narrowing gap and squeezed through.

The Daleks glided in pursuit, gun-sticks blazing, then were hidden from view by the closing door . . .

Bettan tapped the soldier on the arm. He pushed the plunger down with all his force. A thunderous explosion on the other side of the doors shook the checkpoint, sending them all flying.

Sarah picked herself up, and staggered over to the scanner screen. Incredibly, it was still working. On it they could see Daleks in a menacing circle around Davros. Davros was desperately trying to regain control of his creations but they could hear the fear in his voice. 'You must obey me,' he was saying. 'I created you. I am your master!'

One of the Daleks seemed to be speaking for the others, as if already they had evolved their own leaders. 'Our programming does not permit us to acknowledge any creature superior to the Daleks.'

'Without me you cannot exist,' insisted Davros. 'You cannot progress.'

There was total arrogance in the Dalek voice, the arrogance that Davros himself had given it. 'We are programmed to survive. We have the ability to evolve in any way necessary for that survival.'

Another Dalek glided in. Ignoring Davros, it reported to its leader. 'Main exit blocked by explosion to length of one thousand units.'

The Dalek began issuing orders to deal with the problem. Other Daleks glided to obey.

Sarah nudged the Doctor. 'Did you manage to do anything in the Incubator Room?'

'Quite a bit—with a little help from a Dalek. The damage I did will set them back a thousand years.'

'That's pretty good then, isn't it?'

The Doctor smiled ruefully. 'In the totality of Time, it's no more than—that!' and he snapped his fingers.

Harry drew their attention to the screen. 'Look, something's happening.'

Fascinated they gathered round to watch the inevitable end of the clash between Davros and the monsters he had created. The terrified handful of scientists who had elected to support Davros were being herded into a corner. The Dalek leader spoke. 'All inferior creatures are the enemy of the Daleks. They must be destroyed.'

Davros began pleading for the few men who had been loyal to him. 'Wait. These men are scientists. They can help you. Let them live. Have you no pity?'

'Pi-ty?' The word sounded strange in the Dalek voice. 'I have no understanding of the word. It is not registered in my vocabulary bank.' It wheeled to face the other Daleks. 'Exterminate them!' Once again the Dalek gun-sticks roared, and the handful of humans crumpled and fell.

In the centre of the laboratory, Davros confronted the Dalek leader. 'For the last time . . . I am your creator. You must . . . you will . . . obey me!'

'We obey no one. We are the Daleks!'

The watchers saw Davros spin his chair and speed it towards the destructor button on the wall. As his withered hand reached up, they heard the voice of the Dalek leader. 'Exterminate him!' All the Daleks seemed to fire at once, and Davros and his chair exploded in flame, the destructor button still untouched.

The Dalek leader glided forward to address its fellows. The action brought it closer to the scanner screen so that it seemed almost to be talking to the small group watching in the checkpoint. 'We are entombed here, but we still live on. This is only the beginning. We will prepare. We will grow stronger. When the time is right, we will emerge. We shall build our own City. We shall rule Skaro. The Daleks will be the supreme power in the Universe . . .!' Suddenly the screen went blank.

'Thank goodness,' said Sarah. '*Please*—can we go now?'

Sevrin, Bettan and the others were already leaving, assuming the Doctor and his friends would follow them out of the blockhouse.

The Doctor said, 'The Time Ring please, Sarah.'

As Sarah gave him the Ring she said, 'We've failed, haven't we, Doctor?'

'Not entirely. We've given the Daleks a nasty setback, perhaps that's all we were intended to do . . . it's a kind of victory.'

He smiled at Sarah who said, '*You* don't seem too disappointed anyway.'

'Hand on the ring, please,' said the Doctor briskly. He held it up, and Harry and Sarah obeyed. Their fingers touched the metal and after a moment Sarah felt a strange disembodied sensation sweeping over her.

Sevrin, who had come back into the checkpoint to see what was delaying his friends, was astonished to see them simply fading away into nothingness. Sarah waved, called 'Goodbye, Sevrin . . .' and vanished.

Sarah felt everything dissolve into spinning blackness. But somehow she could still hear the Doctor's voice echoing hollowly. 'Disappointed, Sarah? No, not really. You see, although I know that Daleks will create havoc and destruction for untold thousands of years . . . I also know that out of their great evil . . . some . . . great . . . good . . . must come.'

About the Authors

Terrance Dicks

Born in East Ham in London in 1935, Terrance Dicks worked in the advertising industry after leaving university before moving into television as a writer. He worked together with Malcolm Hulke on scripts for *The Avengers* as well as other series before becoming Assistant and later full Script Editor of *Doctor Who* from 1968.

Working closely with friend and series Producer Barry Letts, Dicks worked on the entirety of the Third Doctor's era of the programme starring Jon Pertwee, and returned as a writer – scripting Tom Baker's first story as the Fourth Doctor: *Robot*. He left *Doctor Who* to work first as Script Editor and then as Producer on the BBC's prestigious *Classic Serials*, and to pursue his writing career on screen and in print. His later scriptwriting credits on *Doctor Who* included the twentieth-anniversary story *The Five Doctors* broadcast in 1983.

Terrance Dicks novelised many of the original *Doctor Who* stories for Target books, and discovered a liking and talent for prose fiction. He has written extensively for children, creating such memorable series and characters as T.R. Bear and The Baker Street Irregulars, as well as continuing to write original *Doctor Who* novels for BBC Books.

Terry Nation

Terry Nation was born in 1930 in Llandaff in South Wales. Nation started as a comedy writer and performer, although much of his later drama writing was influenced by his memories of growing up during the Second World War – as he pointed out, the Daleks are based very much on Nazis.

But he quickly realised that he was better at writing than performing, and went on to provide material for various comedians during the 1950s, including Frankie Howerd.

In 1962, Nation scripted three episodes of ABC's *Out of this World* science fiction anthology series. Two were adapted from short stories, but the third was an original work called *Botany Bay*. From this he moved on to write an episode of the series *No Hiding Place*.

While working with comedian Tony Hancock, Nation was approached with an offer to work on *Doctor Who*. He was not initially impressed with the format of the series, but after a falling out with Hancock found himself without work. So he quickly accepted the *Doctor Who* job, hurriedly providing the seven episodes of the first ever Dalek story before moving on to further work.

After inventing the Daleks, Nation worked on several prestigious ITC television series including *The Saint*, *The Baron* (on which he was Script Supervisor), *The Champions*, *The Avengers* (where he became Script Editor), *Department S*, *The Pursuaders!* (as Associate Producer and Story Consultant), and the Gerry Anderson-produced series *The Protectors*.

In the 1970s, Nation was once again working for the BBC. He provided a play starring Robert Hardy as *The Incredible Robert Baldick* which was intended by Nation to be the pilot for a series, although sadly this was never pursued. Following this he scripted four more Dalek series for *Doctor Who* – including *Genesis of the Daleks* which explained the creatures' origins and introduced the character of Davros.

Also in the mid 1970s, Nation created the popular series *Survivors* which depicted a world all but wiped out by plague with the few survivors struggling to cling on to civilisation. The series was revived and updated by the BBC in 2008. Nation later devised the hugely popular BBC science fiction series *Blake's 7*.

Terry Nation and his family moved to Los Angeles in 1980 where he continued to work in television providing scripts and ideas. It was in Los Angeles that Terry Nation died in 1996, aged just 66.